THE BEST MEDICINE

MERCY HOSPITAL
THE BEST MEDICINE

CAROLYN CARLYLE

AN AVON CAMELOT BOOK

MERCY HOSPITAL: THE BEST MEDICINE is an original publication of Avon Books. This work has never before appeared in book form.

AVON BOOKS
A division of
The Hearst Corporation
1350 Avenue of the Americas
New York, New York 10019

Copyright © 1993 by Seth Godin
Published by arrangement with Seth Godin Productions
Library of Congress Catalog Card Number: 92-93927
ISBN: 0-380-76847-X
RL: 5.4

First Avon Camelot Printing: April 1993

CAMELOT TRADEMARK REG. U.S. PAT. OFF. AND IN OTHER COUNTRIES, MARCA REGISTRADA, HECHO EN U.S.A.

Printed in the U.S.A.

OPM   10   9   8   7   6   5   4   3   2   1

Contents

1
Roger the Klutz

The five freshmen filed into Pizza Paradise, Ridge Dale High's most popular after-school hangout. Four of the teenagers slipped into their favorite booth and began talking excitedly about the football game they'd just watched.

A tall, sandy-haired boy stood awkwardly to one side of the noisy group. While the rest gossiped and laughed, he fumbled with the sling on his right arm. Then a slim girl with red hair and lively green eyes made room for him beside her. "Come on, Rog," Bernadette O'Connor urged, smiling. "We've got room for you *and* your cast."

Roger Thornton sat down, then gingerly maneuvered his injured arm underneath the tabletop and slid across the seat. From the other side of the table, Nichole Peters, Shelley Jansen, and Teddy Hollins watched his slow progress. "Boy," laughed Nichole, "it's a good thing you weren't out there with your team today. I don't think you would have been much help!"

Roger looked down at the white plaster sleeve that hid

his elbow and lower arm. It was covered with signatures and silly notes scribbled in ink and magic marker. "I'm glad we won," he admitted, grinning at Nichole, whose blonde hair and flawless makeup looked perfect enough to be on a magazine cover. "But it sure is hard to watch from the stands when you're used to calling the plays."

Beside him, the pretty redhead everyone called Bernie for short nodded. She had been at the game weeks before when the standout JV quarterback had broken his arm. In a way, she felt responsible for Roger's injury. After all, it was Bernie he had turned to wave at during a time-out. He'd been so intent on finding her face in the crowd, he hadn't looked where he was going and had tripped over the water dispenser. No wonder his friends were always teasing him about his clumsiness. And his crush on Bernie!

Bernie touched his cast gently, tapping the place where she'd signed her name in blue. "I know it's not easy," she told him now. "But you've been a great patient."

Roger smiled down at her. "I had a great nurse," he said.

Shelley corrected him. "We're not nurses, Rog." Small, with a dark French braid that trailed down her back, Shelley was best friends with Nichole and Bernie. "The three of us are Junior Volunteers."

"With the emphasis on *volunteers*," Nichole reminded them. "I still can't figure out how Bernie talked us into working at the hospital for nothing!" Everyone knew Nichole was only joking. She loved her new job at Mercy General. She felt special each time she put on the striped uniform she kept in a place of honor among the rows of smart skirts and expensive dresses in her closet at the Peters' mansion.

"You, my loaded beauty," Teddy Hollins told her, "are the very last person in the world who should complain about her salary." Skinny, with an angular face and the

2

latest punk haircut, Teddy winked at Nichole to show he was just teasing.

But Nichole, the only daughter of one of Ridge Dale's wealthiest families, didn't see the humor in Teddy's clowning. She pointed a manicured finger at him accusingly. "If you think I've got it so easy, Mr. Hollins, why don't *you* try buying this year's fashions with last year's allowance."

Bernie shook her head. She knew how flighty and spoiled Nichole could seem. But she also knew that, when it counted, Nichole was a warm and honest friend, and one of the best volunteers Mercy had. "All I know," she said, "is that you're not winning your service pin for your wardrobe, Nick."

"Can you believe we've already worked thirty-five hours at the hospital?" Shelley asked. "I can't wait for the pinning ceremony on Monday."

"Me, too." Bernie sighed with satisfaction. Somehow, two months ago, it seemed like the three of them would never come this far. "Remember how your dad laid down the law, Shell? How he said you couldn't afford to do volunteer work?"

Shelley, whose divorced father worked hard to support them, shuddered when she thought how close she'd come to having to give up her exciting job at Mercy. "You all saved my life," she told the others, "when you came up with that catering scheme." Now, thanks to encouragement from her friends, Shelley, who loved to cook, sold her gourmet treats to the hospital snack bar and made enough money to really help out at home.

"Hey," added Nichole, "you aren't the only one who nearly lost her job at Mercy." She smiled her cover-girl smile at her two best friends. "Remember what a lousy volunteer I was at first?"

"I wouldn't say you were lousy," Bernie told her. She

3

recalled the way Nichole had run from the sight of blood, the way she'd hated the idea of touching or talking to sick people. "I'd say you were horrendous!"

For once, Nichole took the teasing in stride. "You're right," she admitted, grinning. "I was too busy being scared to think about how scared the patients were." She thought back to her first visit to Mercy's Long Term Care Unit. She could still picture the way an elderly woman's face had broken into a happy smile when Nichole had pinned a flower on her hospital gown. That was when she had finally learned what being a volunteer was all about.

"Well, I wasn't about to give up my job at Mercy," Bernie reminded her friends. She looked up at the handsome boy beside her. "But working there almost cost me one of my very best friends."

Roger flushed, staring into his nearly empty soda glass. "Boy, was I off the mark," he told Bernie. "I really acted like a jerk when you three started working at Mercy." He paused until he gathered the courage to look straight into Bernie's wide, lime-colored eyes. "It's just that I was afraid it would break up our group. I really counted on meeting you all after practice, hanging out together on weekends.

"But then my accident landed me in the hospital. And I guess it's just what I deserved," he admitted sheepishly. "I got a chance to see firsthand the important job you all do." He shook his head, regretting every hard, unkind remark he'd made about the girls' "good samaritan routine."

Sandwiched between Shelley and Nichole, Teddy grinned at his athletic pal. "That hospital stay would have changed *anybody's* mind," he announced. "After all, major jock here had three irresistible females waiting on him hand and foot!" He remembered the way the girls had scrambled to sign Roger's cast, the way they had taken

4

turns feeding him in the hospital. "Life's just not fair," he complained. "I should have broken my arm instead. That way, Roger could still be playing football, and I could be basking in nonstop attention."

"No way, Super Ego," Nichole told him in an icy tone. "You'd have to break every bone in your body before I'd lift a finger."

"You're just saying that to conceal the storm of passion you feel each time we're together." Teddy couldn't resist watching gorgeous Nichole lose her cool.

"Storm of passion?" Nichole turned on him, her blue eyes flashing. "There's only one passion you unleash in me, Teddy Hollins. And that's a passion to tear you limb from limb."

"That's a start," the class cutup told her. He grinned hopefully. "We can build from there."

"Ohhhhh!" Nichole squeezed as far away from Teddy as she could in the narrow booth, then glanced toward the heavyset man headed toward their table with a round tray. "If our Paradise Deluxe hadn't just arrived, I'd be out of here!"

"Thank goodness for pepperoni," announced Bernie, laughing, as the man placed a huge pizza in front of them. "It's the great peacemaker." All the teens reached for slices of the steaming pie. "Okay, everyone," Shelley added, "dive into your wallets. Peace and pepperoni aren't free."

"Excuse me, Miss," their waiter interrupted. "But this pizza's on the house."

"What?" The five friends stared at each other. Ever since they'd started at Ridge Dale that fall, they'd been coming to Pizza Paradise after school. They loved the winged slices of pizza painted on the ceiling, the soft crust on the Deluxe, and the way no one bothered them when they sat talking and laughing there for hours. But, in all

5

the time they'd been coming here, no one had ever offered them a free pizza!

"Mr. Calante, the owner, told me this Deluxe is the least he can do for his son Jason's favorite nurse." The waiter put a napkin and plate in front of each teen, then excused himself.

"Jason?" Shelley's eyes lit up as she repeated the name. "Jason Calante?" Her sunny smile made it plain that Jason was someone special. She turned to Nichole, then Bernie. "Don't you remember that little boy in Pediatrics? The one who'd had a tonsillectomy?"

"Of course!" Bernie said. "Your not-so-secret admirer, Shell!" Bernie recalled the tow-headed youngster who'd taken such a liking to Shelley when the three girls had been assigned to "Peeds," Mercy's unit for children. The little boy, whose parents were out of town, had begged Shelley to read him the same story over and over.

"Sure!" added Nichole, remembering, too. "The floor nurse said you could stay with Jason while Bernie and I had to spend our time making yucky beds!"

"Do you mean that little boy's dad owns Pizza Paradise?" asked Teddy.

"I guess so," Shelley said, her chocolate-colored eyes still shining. "He was absolutely the cutest, most adorable little guy ever."

"Say," suggested Teddy, calculating the chances of more free pie, "is he in good health?" He paused, grinning. "I mean, do you think there's a chance he might have to go back to Mercy again soon?"

"Teddy Hollins!" scolded Bernie. "Bite your tongue." She smiled at their goofy friend. "Or at least bite your Deluxe and save the drama for your movies."

Teddy, who planned on studying film in college, was determined to be a famous movie director when he grew up. He carried a video camera with him almost everywhere. And, whether they liked it or not, his friends were the subjects of most of his "docudramas."

Now Teddy, who'd left his camera at home, held his fingers in a frame in front of his face. Then he trained his imaginary camera on Nichole. "Wait," he shouted. "Let me catch this with the old air camera." He panned up and down. "This is quite a moment," he declared, keeping Nichole in focus as she chewed her slice of Deluxe. "I think I'll call this *The Blonde who Devoured Cleveland.*"

"That does it!" Nichole put her pie down and pried Teddy's fingers apart. "If you don't stop that this instant, Lame Brain, you won't live long enough to be a director." She turned in her seat and began to pull on the silver hoop that hung from Teddy's right ear.

Teddy writhed as she pulled harder and harder on his earring. "Okay! Okay!" He sat up in relief as she stopped, rubbing his red ear.

"Just don't go filming people without permission," Nichole told him, picking up her pizza and nibbling it daintily.

"Hey," Roger said, "at least my man Teddy knows what he wants out of life." He wrapped his arm around Teddy now. Even though the two were as different as could be, they were the best of friends. "Not like me," he added, sounding depressed.

"What's up, Rog?" Bernie asked.

"I don't know." Roger leaned back in the booth, propping his cast on the table. "It's just that I feel so . . . so . . . useless, I guess."

"What do you mean?" Shelley was surprised to hear Roger feeling sorry for himself.

"Well, you all have your work at the hospital, and Teddy's always making films—but what do I do?" He shifted uncomfortably in his seat. "I mean ever since the accident,

7

I can't play football, I can't write, I can barely feed myself."

"But your cast will be off in a week," Nichole told him. The whole gang had been counting the days until they could give Roger his "cast party." "Then everything will be back to normal."

"No it won't," Roger told her. "Normal for me is practice every day and games on weekends." He looked at his friends, then lowered his eyes to the table. "This arm means I'm out for the season. I've got to sit on the sidelines while you guys do the things you care about, the things you're good at. The only thing I'm good at is football."

"That's not true!" Bernie could hardly believe this was the calm, confident boy she knew. "Why, you're one of the most popular, busiest people I know."

"Not anymore." Roger slumped in his seat, determined not to be cheered up.

"If you're good for nothing," suggested Nichole with a smile, "how come you were elected to the student council?"

"That's just because I play football," Roger told her. "They figure they need at least one dumb jock to represent us."

Shelley rolled her eyes. "If you're such a dumb jock," she asked, "how come you always get better grades on your math tests than I do?" Shelley and Roger were both in Mrs. Vickers' algebra class, and the little, bespectacled woman made a habit of handing back test papers in order, best grades to worst. Shelley was tired of being stuck in the middle, six or seven papers behind her friend.

"The only reason I keep my grades up," Roger explained, "is because Coach makes us." He took a last, slow sip of soda, then pushed his uneaten slice of Deluxe

8

away. "It's the only way I can play football. And, let's face it, I don't have anything else to do."

"Negativo, good buddy." Teddy wasn't about to let his friend stay down in the dumps. "As I recall, you made a promise to these fair damsels while you were flat on your back in the hospital."

"I did?" Roger had clearly forgotten his promise. But the person who'd asked him to make it hadn't.

"That's right!" Bernie looked gratefully at Teddy. "Remember, Rog? You promised me that when your arm was better you'd think about being a JV with the rest of us."

"A Junior Volunteer? *Me?*" Roger laughed, embarrassed. "That's sort of like asking a bear to thread a needle, isn't it?" He studied the plaster cast, remembering the way he'd tripped over his own feet at the game. "I mean, I'm not exactly the picture of grace."

"You'll do just fine." Bernie was sure their warm, handsome friend would make a great addition to the hospital's staff. She could picture him chatting with patients, moving stretchers, and pushing wheelchairs. "And we need all the help we can get with Thanksgiving coming up."

"We sure do," agreed Nichole. "That's when patients get really blue and need lots of TLC."

"I know how they feel," Roger told her. "Thanksgiving's going to be a bad time for me, too." All Roger's friends knew how much he'd been looking forward to the biggest football game of the year.

"Talk about Thanksgiving blues!" moaned Shelley. "I've got an order from Mercy's snack bar for one hundred fifty pumpkin pies and fifty mincemeat tarts." She popped the last bite of Deluxe into her mouth. "At this rate, I'll be cooking for the rest of my life!"

"No, you won't," Bernie told her. "Not with your four ace assistant cooks here."

9

"Four?" Teddy looked doubtful. "I'm an artist, not a kitchen worker!"

"Great," Nichole said. "You can help me decorate the pies."

"Hmmmm." Teddy considered her proposition. "It's a deal. As long as we work *very closely* together." Teddy wrote in imaginary letters across an imaginary screen. "Yes, I can see it now. *Honey, I Froze the Whipped Cream,* a cinematic triumph directed by Theodore Hollins, written by Theodore Hollins, starring Theodore Hollins . . ."

"Hey!" Nichole interrupted. "Whose idea was this, anyway?"

Teddy grinned. "Okay, okay." He started writing again. "And in a small, supporting role, introducing Nichole Peters."

Nichole pushed Teddy into Shelley, who pushed him back. "You are utterly hopeless, Teddy Hollins," Nichole announced. Then she stood up, straightening her suede miniskirt. "Come on everyone, it's time for some *real* movies. I rented two Corey Hudson films, and I can't wait to see that gorgeous face of his spread across our big-screen TV."

Everytime it was Nichole's turn to rent Saturday videos for the gang, she picked movies featuring her favorite star. Bernie thought that by now they must have watched every movie Corey Hudson had ever made. "Okay," she sighed. "But next time, let's let someone else pick the movie."

As the teens stood and headed toward the door, Nichole considered Bernie's suggestion. "Just as long as it isn't one of the guys who picks," she agreed. "If I have to sit through one more kung fu epic, I'll scream."

Just as he had when they'd come in, Roger trailed behind the rest of his friends. He clearly had something besides videos on his mind. "Do you really think I could make the grade at Mercy?" he asked Bernie.

Bernie turned, smiling. "Of course you could." She dropped back to fall in step with him. "Working at Mercy is the most exciting, important thing I've ever done." She touched his shoulder. "And if you're worried about fitting in, why not come with us to the pinning ceremony Monday night? You could meet some of the other kids who volunteer."

"I don't know. I'm not sure."

Now Shelley dropped behind the rest of the group to second the suggestion. "Oh, come on, Rog. It'd be fun to have you with us." She laughed, remembering all the mistakes she'd made in training. "Everyone worries about messing up at first, but I know you'll do just fine."

"Well, I guess I could come to the ceremony," Roger told her. "It's not like I've got football practice or anything."

"Great!" Bernie winked at Shelley. "It's decided. Everyone, I'd like you to meet Mercy Hospital's newest JV."

Nichole and Teddy turned, and Roger made an awkward bow from the waist. As he did, his cast hit the edge of a pizza tray that was set on the counter by the door. In an instant, the tray had clattered to the floor, sending sausage and olives and gooey pizza in all directions at once.

"Roger the Klutz strikes again!" Nichole couldn't help herself. Laughing, she held her hands over her mouth.

As a waiter rushed over with a rag, Teddy stared at the colorful disaster on the floor. "Hmmm," he said. "I think we should skip the olives next time."

"See, I told you," Roger said, depressed all over again. "I couldn't make it at Mercy. What if that was a tray full of bandages or medicine or something?"

"Hey, that was just a silly accident," Shelley assured

him. "You're the most coordinated person I've ever seen when it comes to football plays."

"But off the field," Roger insisted, "Nichole's right. I'm Roger the Klutz."

"Nonsense," Bernie said firmly. "You've just got the JV jitters. Nichole got them. I got them. You'll do fine." She took his arm, steering him out the door into the crisp fall air. "In fact, I bet you'll be one of the best volunteers ever."

The boys and girls filed out into the street and headed toward the Peters' mansion. As they walked along, chatting and laughing, Bernie wondered: Would Roger really fit in at Mercy? Was he just suffering from beginner's nerves—or could his clumsiness cause a lot more damage than spilled pizza?

2

Mrs. Nobody

It was late when the gang's Saturday night "movie party" ended and Bernie headed home. As she walked into the cheerful living room of the O'Connors' Victorian house, she could tell that her baby brother and her three younger sisters were already in bed. Their toys and books had been tucked into the cubbies that lined the walls, and her parents were reading quietly on the sofa.

Bernie was glad. She loved her big, noisy family, but sometimes she needed time alone with her parents. Mary and Frank O'Connor had a way of helping her think things through. And right now she had something on her mind.

Bernie's mother, a young-looking woman with the same pale skin and green eyes as her daughter, looked up at her and smiled. Bernie's father, a robust, handsome man, whose dark hair was just beginning to gray, put down the latest issue of *Tennis Talk* magazine as Bernie sank into a chair opposite them. "What's up, Princess?" he asked.

Mr. O'Connor, who helped coach Ridge Dale's tennis

13

team, thought about the sport all year round. But even though his wife sometimes joked about being a "tennis widow," everyone knew his family came first. Which was why Bernie could never hide her worries from her dad. He leaned forward now, studying his eldest daughter's face. "It looks like you've been working on a problem."

"It's not really a problem," Bernie explained. "It's more like I'm borrowing trouble before it happens."

"Well, if you're borrowing trouble," her father said, standing, tousling Bernie's red hair, "why not borrow a little free advice while you're at it?" He headed toward the kitchen. "I'll heat up some tea and we'll have a talk."

Bernie's mother folded the newspaper she'd been reading. "I guess we all borrow trouble sometimes," she said. "For instance, right now I'm picturing your father making that tea." She cocked her head, trying to see into the kitchen. "You know how he likes to load up on sugar."

From the other room, they heard the banging of cupboards and the clinking of china. When Bernie's father returned, he was carrying a tray loaded with a teapot and three ceramic mugs. He set everything on the table and began pouring them each a cup of steaming tea. When he finished, he lifted his own glass and took a long sip. "Hmmmmmm," he said appreciatively. "Just the way I like it." Bernie and her mother exchanged I-told-you-so glances.

Mr. O'Connor resumed his place on the couch, then turned to Bernie. "Drink up, Princess," he suggested. "Dr. O'Connor's magic elixir is guaranteed to melt problems away."

Bernie took a cautious sip. She tasted one quarter tea and three quarters sugar. Quickly she put her mug down. "What's wrong?" Mr. O'Connor asked. "Need more sugar?"

Mrs. O'Connor and Bernie burst out laughing. "No,

14

Dad," Bernie said, putting a hand over her mug. "No, thanks."

"At least, it's good to see you laughing," her father observed.

"It sure is," Mrs. O'Connor agreed. "You looked so glum when you came in. I expected you'd be on cloud nine—after all, you've got the pinning ceremony day after tomorrow." She touched her daughter's arm, smiling. "We're both proud of you, Honey."

"Thanks, Mom." Bernie had to admit that she felt proud and excited about Monday, too. She couldn't wait to hang the little silver thirty-five from the hospital pin on her uniform. It meant she'd made it. She'd worked thirty-five hours and she was a full-fledged hospital volunteer!

"So, why so serious?" Mrs. O'Connor asked.

"It's Roger," Bernie admitted. "I've talked him into something he may not be ready for."

"What's that?" Mr. O'Connor put his empty glass on the tray.

"Volunteering at Mercy," Bernie told them.

"That's wonderful," Bernie's mother said. "From what I hear, Mercy is really understaffed right now. The more help the doctors and nurses can get, the better."

"Sure." Bernie nodded. "It's just that Roger is worried about making mistakes. You know how clumsy he can be."

Mrs. O'Connor remembered Roger's visits—and the broken dishes and overturned chairs he left behind each time he set foot in the house. "Well," she agreed, smiling, "he's not exactly ballet material."

"But he doesn't need to be," Bernie's father assured them. "All he needs is his heart in the right place. Besides," he went on, "remember how worried you were about Nichole? How scared she was of being a volun-

15

teer?'' He settled back in the couch. ''And she came through with flying colors.''

''That's right,'' Mary O'Connor agreed, standing, the tray of tea things in her hand. ''Your clumsy young man may surprise you with his grace under pressure.''

''Maybe,'' said Bernie, hopefully. As she kissed her mom and dad good night, she felt better. After all, she reminded herself, Roger *was* graceful as could be when he played football. Going upstairs, she thought about how depressed he'd been, how badly he needed to feel useful. Maybe that's all it would take, she thought. Just put him where a job needs to be done. A few minutes later, falling asleep under the glow-in-the-dark stars she'd pasted to her bedroom ceiling years ago, Bernie pictured working side by side with Roger, doing something worthwhile. Something they both loved.

Bernie usually hated Mondays. It was hard to get used to classes and homework again after the weekend. But this Monday was different. There was a special excitement in the air when the gang met for lunch in Ridge Dale's steamy, crowded cafeteria. ''I stayed up all night baking,'' Shelley told her friends over the noise. ''Mrs. Hurley asked me to come up with refreshments to serve after we get our pins.''

''So, what did you concoct, oh genius of gastronomy?'' Teddy had joined the girls for lunch at their regular table. ''I sure hope it's better than Ridge Dale's mystery meat.'' He covered his eyes with one hand, and with the other poked a fork into the food on his tray.

''Come on, Teddy,'' Bernie said. ''Ridge Dale's food doesn't look as bad as it tastes.'' She pushed her tray away, laughing, and sipped her Coke instead. ''And what was that fancy name you just called Shelley?''

''Genius of gastronomy,'' Teddy told her. ''How come

16

Miss Straight A's doesn't know 'gastronomy' means cooking?''

"How come Mr. C- is flashing around fifty-dollar words?" Roger, who'd stayed late copying a monster math homework problem from the board with his left hand, joined them at the table. He grinned at his friend. "Is the Tedster turning over a new leaf?"

Teddy seemed embarrassed. "No," he said. "It's just that Miss Prince, our substitute English teacher, says there's nothing more compelling than a good vocabulary."

"Let me guess." Roger studied his pal with a knowing smile. "Miss Prince wouldn't happen to be terrific looking, would she?"

"Absolutely not," insisted Nichole, who'd seen the new sub in the halls that morning. "Her hairstyle is straight out of the '70's. And if that outfit she has on today is her idea of style, she's hopelessly out of touch."

"Hey, wait just a minute," Teddy warned her. "I wouldn't say that pinafore you're wearing is exactly high fashion."

Everyone stopped to stare at Nichole, who wore her striped hospital tunic over a white blouse. Although it was very different from the rest of her expensive clothes, the simple tunic brought out her striking good looks. She shook her blonde head. "I don't care what anybody thinks," she said proudly. "I'm working at Mercy after school, and I positively refuse to rumple this darling outfit by stuffing it in my locker all day."

"That's right," confirmed Bernie. "Nick has started a whole new trend. All the other volunteers were afraid to wear their uniforms to school until she started doing it."

"Yep," added Shelley. "We didn't want to get teased to death." She winked at her friend. "But you know Nick. She makes fashions, she doesn't follow them."

17

Bernie put her arm around her friend. "Do you think you'll be able to get your nose out of the dictionary long enough to attend that pinning ceremony tonight, Teddy?"

"Attend?" Teddy asked. "Of course, I'm attending. In fact, I'm going to be your official photographer. I'm bringing my still *and* my video cameras to record this momentous occasion."

"Hey," Shelley insisted. "It isn't *that* big a deal. The whole thing's only going to last fifteen minutes."

"Fifteen minutes that will live forever," Teddy told her. "Immortalized on film."

"You're coming, too, aren't you, Rog?" Nichole asked. "Maybe you can keep Steven Spielberg here from embarrassing us all." She stood up, smoothing the skirt of her crisp, pin-striped uniform, then turned to Bernie and Shelley. "Or better yet, while I'm on duty at Mercy, maybe you two could talk him out of coming." She scooped up her tray as the bell for sixth period rang.

The others gathered up their trays and followed her toward the conveyor belt at the rear of the cafeteria. "I'll be there," Roger assured her as they piled their trays onto the belt. He looked down at Bernie, who stood beside him. "I wouldn't miss it."

Nichole, who helped out in Mercy's flower room after school on Mondays, met her friends outside the hospital's Volunteer Office at seven that night. Looking tired but happy, she led them to a table loaded with trays of cookies, a silver punch bowl, and tiny glass cups. "Isn't this too wonderful?" she asked. "Mrs. Hurley brought in all her own silver and I did the centerpiece."

Sure enough, in the middle of the table was a cut glass bowl filled with delicate sprays of hollyhocks and carnations. "You did a great job—as always," Bernie told her warmly.

"And these cookies taste great, Shell," added Teddy, who had grabbed one of the treats and was already munching.

Nichole slapped his hand. "Those are for *after* the ceremony," she told him sternly. "Shelley didn't work all day yesterday so you could devour everything before our guests arrive."

"But I *am* a guest," Teddy insisted.

"So am I," added Roger, looking longingly at the chocolate-studded cookies.

"Okay," relented Nichole, handing them each a cookie. "But wait for seconds until the others get here."

"Looks like they're already here," Bernie announced, as three more teenagers walked in with their parents. A handsome black boy with broad shoulders and an easy smile waved at them. "You remember Blake Willard, Rog?" Bernie smiled as the two boys shook hands.

Blake, the captain of Hayward High's varsity football and wrestling teams, clapped Roger on the back. "My man," he said, grinning. "The last time I saw you, you were horizontal." Blake, who volunteered at Mercy with the girls, had served on the Orthopedics Unit the day Roger was hurt. "Looks like you'll be ready for ball next season."

"Maybe," said Roger, smiling in spite of himself. "It's not much fun on the sidelines."

Blake had a way with people, always knowing how to make them feel good about themselves. "You'll be practicing in no time," he said. "Meanwhile, I'll bet there's a lot you could do." He looked at the others. "Couldn't we use an extra volunteer, guys?"

"There's always room for one more," a cheerful voice interrupted them. "I'm Pat Hurley, Mercy's Director of Volunteers," announced a small woman as she joined the

19

group. She had a frank, relaxed manner that put everyone at ease. "When can you start?"

Roger laughed. "As soon as this cast's off, I guess," he told her. "I've got lots of free time."

"And we can use every bit of it, right, team?" Pat Hurley smiled at the teens. After Bernie had introduced Teddy and Roger to her, she greeted each of her volunteers in turn, meeting their parents and thanking them for coming. Besides Blake, the star athlete, there was Clifford Foster, a shy, blond boy who also went to Hayward. Clifford had two passions—debate and volunteering. Then there was Julie Hayden, a tall, slender girl from East Wood High who'd become great friends with Nichole, Shelley, and Bernie.

"It's neat to meet everyone's parents," Shelley whispered to her friends. "Sort of a preview of coming attractions."

"I know what you mean," giggled Nichole. "Look at Clifford's dad—he looks just like a grown-up nerd."

"Nichole Peters!" scolded Bernie. "How can you talk like that? Especially when Cliff has such a crush on you!"

Nichole shrugged. "I like Cliff, too," she said. "He's taught me how nice nerds can be."

Julie joined them. "Hi, guys," she said. "Isn't this great? Where are your parents? Couldn't they come?"

"My dad works nights," Shelley explained.

"My parents are in Europe," Nichole added.

"My mom and dad are late," said Bernie, looking anxiously toward the main door. "I wish they'd get here."

As if on cue, the O'Connor family walked into the room. Frank and Mary led the rest of their children: ten-year-old Tracy, a pretty youngster with a bouncy red ponytail; Sara, who was seven and had hair as red as her two older sisters'; Kelly, who was five and the only O'Connor with black curls; and their baby brother, Matt, who raced

20

toward the cookie trays and grabbed two from each before his sisters could stop him.

The entire group stood and chatted, the parents comparing notes, full of questions for Mrs. Hurley. But after a few minutes, the Volunteer Director excused herself and walked to a small table set up in the back of the room. "Okay, everyone," she said. "I'd like to say just a few words about these special volunteers of mine." Everyone quieted and looked toward her.

"It's not always easy to be a Junior Volunteer," she continued. "For one thing, there's a lot going on in a teenager's life—it's hard to fit the hospital in when you've got school, home, friends, and dating to think about.

"Then there's peer pressure." Pat Hurley knew how often her young staff got teased about being do-gooders. "When you want to help others, that sometimes makes you seem different." She reached into a box on the table and pulled out a tiny white card with a small gold pin and chain attached to it. "But I'm here to tell you that being different is how the world gets changed. Anyone who says kids don't care hasn't met the kids in this room."

She smiled as the parents and families burst into applause. "Clifford Foster, would you step forward," she asked. Cliff, his face blushing violently under his light hair, walked up beside her. She had removed the pin from its card, and now she gently pinned it onto the hospital blazer Cliff had worn to the ceremony. "Julie Hayden, would you come up?"

In turn, each of the teens was called forward, and each received a small pin shaped like the number thirty-five. Mrs. Hurley fastened it into place so that it hung just underneath the shiny Mercy Hospital service pin each volunteer wore on his or her uniform. As Bernie looked down at the tiny gold lamb and lion nestled together on her Mercy pin, then at the sparkling thirty-five beneath it, she

21

felt very proud. "You've all done more than *try* volunteering," Mrs. Hurley told them now. "You've proved you're serious. You've made time in your life for Mercy. And the staff and patients all thank you for it."

There was more applause, and Bernie flashed a smile at her family—especially at toddler Matt, who held his last cookie in his mouth, while he clapped loudly with both hands. Then she caught Roger's eye. He was applauding, too, and she thought she saw a special apology in his look—a sweet expression that was meant to tell her he was sorry that he'd once been one of the people who laughed at JVs.

Throughout the brief ceremony, Teddy was busy filming. Even afterward, as the group stood talking and finishing Shelley's cookies and punch, he continued to snap pictures of everyone. "Boy," said Nichole, ignoring him as he zoomed in for a close-up, "Mrs. Hurley sure made me feel better about being a volunteer."

"Better?" Julie and Shelley and Bernie clustered around her. "What do you mean, Nichole?"

"Well, I didn't want to spoil our party, so I didn't mention it before." Nichole, the girls noticed now, didn't look as excited as the rest of them. "I had kind of a bad experience with a patient this afternoon."

"You did?" Bernie couldn't imagine confident Nichole having trouble with anyone. But she saw her friend's worried look. "Who was it, Nick?"

"She wouldn't tell me her name," Nichole said. "She was a sweet-looking old lady on Long Term Care. I couldn't read the name on her water pitcher, so I asked her to pronounce it for me." Nichole's pretty blue eyes darkened at the memory. "All she said was, 'I'm nobody. Just call me Mrs. Nobody.' "

"Maybe she was joking," offered Shelley. "Some of

those seniors have a real sense of humor—that's why I like working on Long Term.''

"She wasn't joking," Nichole said quietly. "She was crying. There were tears in her eyes. I asked the floor nurse, and she said the old woman hardly ever talks to anyone. All the staff knows about her is that she was transferred from the Ridge Dale Nursing Home and that she never has any visitors.''

"That's awful." Bernie knew how lonely some of the older patients without families could get. "What's her room number, Nick? Even if Shelley and I don't get assigned to that Unit tomorrow, we'll pay a special visit when we get off work.''

Nichole brightened. "Thanks," she said, hopefully. "She's in room 308." Then her smile faded. "But I don't think you'll have much luck," she added. "All Mrs. Nobody did the whole time I was with her was stare out the window by her bed. I made her a gorgeous corsage, I told jokes, I even showed her how to blend lipstick shades.'' Nichole sighed. "Nothing worked. Mrs. Nobody wouldn't even talk to me.''

"Don't worry," Bernie said, wrapping her arm around Shelley. "The dynamic duo here will have Mrs. Nobody chatting away in no time." She hoped she was right. She was already curious about this mysterious, sad old woman. She couldn't help wondering what she and Shelley would find when they knocked on the door of room 308.

23

3

The Cast Party

"She doesn't look tragic." whispered Shelley the next afternoon. Peering through the door into room 308, she and Bernie saw a sweet-faced woman sitting in the bed by the window. She had gray hair and was wearing a pretty, blue flannel nightgown.

"Well," Bernie reminded her, "we didn't come up here to look at Mrs. Nobody. We came to talk to her." She took a deep breath, pushed open the door, and walked into the room, Shelley behind her.

"Hi," she said, as the woman turned toward them. "I'm Bernadette O'Connor and this is Shelley Jansen. Would you mind two visitors?"

The woman's pale brown eyes studied them for a minute, then she turned away and stared out the window toward the hospital parking lot. "We're friends of Nichole," Bernie explained. "She's the Volunteer who talked with you yesterday."

The woman turned her back on them without answering.

Shelley and Bernie exchanged nervous glances. "We were just on duty in Hemo today," Shelley tried. "So we thought we'd stop by and say hello."

"Hemo?" The woman turned ever so slightly. "Hemo?" she asked again in a quavering voice.

Bernie knew that hospital shorthand sometimes confused patients. "I'm sorry," she said. "Hemo means Hemodialysis." She remembered the description Mrs. Hurley had given them during training. "That's the unit where outpatients with kidney problems come to get treated."

The woman turned around completely now, and looked both her visitors in the eye. "I know," she said.

"You do?" Bernie and Shelley were surprised.

"Of course," Mrs. Nobody told them firmly. "I'm a nurse." She sat up straight and, for a second, her eyes flashed with pride. But then an empty look swept over them. "Or at least I *used* to be a nurse," she said. Now her whole body seemed to sink back into itself and she turned sadly to the window again.

Bernie and Shelley looked at each other. "You were a *nurse?*" Bernie could hardly believe that the quiet woman in front of them had once moved efficiently in and out of hospital rooms, helping doctors treat patients, administering medication, and monitoring dozens of cases at a time. "Which hospital did you work at?"

Mrs. Nobody tilted her head to one side, as if she were seeing people and things that Bernie and Shelley couldn't. "I didn't work in a hospital," she told them. "We didn't have units and specialties, and we certainly didn't have Candy Stripers like you." She turned her gaze on the two girls, and for the first time, smiled. "Although we sure could have used your help!"

"Candy Stripers?" Shelley looked confused. "We're Junior Volunteers."

Mrs. Nobody smiled again. "In my day, you would

25

have been called Candy Stripers.'' She pointed to Shelley's red and white striped tunic. ''And if you take a look at that uniform you're wearing, you'll see why.''

Bernie and Shelley looked down at the starched fronts of their tunics. It was true! The stripes did look like the pattern on candy canes or lollipops!

''But how could you be a nurse and not work in a hospital?'' asked Bernie. She sat down on a chair opposite Mrs. Nobody, her face bright with curiosity. ''Why didn't you have help?''

''I was a nurse during the war, dear,'' the old woman told her. ''A Red Cross nurse. We moved right behind the troops. Sometimes our operating room was a tent. Sometimes we had to use prayers instead of penicillin.''

''How exciting!'' Shelley sat down beside Bernie, squeezing into the narrow chair along with her friend. ''It sounds just like television!'' she said, bursting to hear more. ''I remember when Hawkeye ran out of anaesthetic on *MASH*.''

Mrs. Nobody shook her head and then she actually laughed. ''I wasn't in the Korean War, dear. It was World War Two.'' Again she shook her head, and again she seemed to be seeing pictures of the past. ''We were a lot surer of what we were fighting for then. But we had a lot fewer supplies and a lot more casualties.''

Visiting hour flew by. Bernie and Shelley had question after question to ask. Mrs. Nobody told them about emergencies, about dying and bleeding young soldiers, about nurses and doctors who laughed and joked to keep from crying. Her stories were much more interesting and suspenseful than anything they'd read or heard. And they were all true!

When the floor nurse stuck her head in the door to announce that visiting was over, it was hard to tell which of the three people in room 308 was more disappointed.

26

"Do we have to go?" Bernie asked. "We want to hear more," Shelley begged.

The floor nurse smiled. "I'm afraid Mrs. Bandler needs her rest."

Mrs. Nobody looked indignant. "What do I need my rest for?" she asked. "To get in shape for sitting around the nursing home card room all day?"

"Now, Mrs. Bandler . . ." the nurse protested.

"Don't 'Mrs. Bandler' me," the old woman told her. Her eyes were losing their sparkle, and the lively flush was fading from her cheeks. "I told you before. I'm not Harriet Bandler anymore. I'm just Mrs. Nobody."

"How can you say that?" Bernie asked. "Why, you were a war nurse. Your life was exciting enough to fill a whole book!"

"Was," said Mrs. Bandler. "It *was* exciting. Now it's full of other old men and women waiting to die."

"What do you mean?" Shelley asked. "I see the shuttle bus from the Ridge Dale Nursing Home in town all the time. I thought they had tons of trips and activities."

Harriet Bandler turned toward the window again. "They do," she said quietly. "If you like crocheting or scrabble or visits to the Aquarium." She sighed. "But if you want to feel useful, they haven't got anything to offer at all." She folded her hands and put them in her lap. "They don't have a game to make life worth living again."

"But," interrupted Bernie, "there must be something . . ."

"I'm afraid you really have to go now," the floor nurse told Shelley and Bernie.

"Thank you, girls," Mrs. Nobody said behind them. She turned from the window, and they could see a single tear working its way down her left cheek. "Thanks for helping me feel alive again. Even if it was only for a little while." She waved sadly, then turned back to the window.

27

"We're on duty again in a few days," Shelley told her.

"Yes," Bernie added eagerly. "We'll be back to see you soon."

But Mrs. Nobody didn't answer. She sat like a statue with her back to the girls as they walked off down the hall.

Bernie and Nichole and Shelley spent the next day planning Roger's "cast party." Sprawled across the O'Connors' living-room floor after school, the three friends cut out invitations in the shape of white arm casts, then wrote the good news across them in magic marker: "Roger's Our Right-Hand Man Again! Come to the Cast Party!"

Even though she was happy for Roger, Bernie couldn't stop thinking about her new friend at Mercy. "I'm glad we're all on duty together tomorrow," she told Nichole. "I can't wait for you to hear Mrs. Nobody's—I mean, Mrs. Bandler's—stories about Red Cross nursing."

Nichole moved her lips like a child as she guided her scissors around the outline of a cast she'd drawn on construction paper. "I can't believe you actually got her to talk," she said. "And I can't believe she was a Red Cross nurse. It's just too romantic!"

"I know," said Shelley, taking the cutout from Nichole and reaching for a green marker from the pile of pens and crayons Bernie had emptied onto the floor. "You should have seen how lively she looked when she described the field hospitals."

"And how depressed she got when she talked about the nursing home," Bernie added. "It's funny, but she and Roger have a lot in common right now."

"What do you mean?" Nichole looked puzzled. "What could young Mr. Jock and old Mrs. Nobody possibly have in common?"

Bernie unfolded an invitation and began writing on the

inside. "Well," she explained, filling in the date and time of the party, "they both feel useless and sorry for themselves." She closed the invitation, and picked up another from the pile Nichole was cutting. "And they both miss doing what they do best."

"That's where the similarity ends," Shelley reminded them. "After he gets his cast off on Saturday, Roger will be on the mend." She thought of Mrs. Nobody sitting by the window. "But I don't see how Mrs. Bandler can ever be a nurse again."

Bernie opened the last invitation. *Saturday, eight P.M.,* she wrote in neat script. *Music, Feasting, and Fun at the O'Connors'.* She sighed. "We've just got to do something," she said. "Mrs. Bandler is too smart and funny to spend all her time playing gin rummy in an old folks' home."

"Well, I'm too smart to have to do history homework," Nichole announced, standing and brushing scraps of paper from her lap. "Mr. Haggerty just doesn't know it yet." She grinned, grabbing her books from the hall table. Mr. Haggerty was the newest teacher on Ridge Dale's faculty, but his students were already complaining about the way he piled on reading assignments. "I'll see you two in school tomorrow. We've got zillions of invitations to give out!"

It was true. There were invitations to hand out in school and so many details to plan, that Bernie forgot about Mrs. Bandler until the next afternoon when the three friends had finished work at Mercy. After a shift on the Med-Surg Unit, they were exhausted, but anxious to stop by room 308 in Long Term Care. Sure enough, their elderly friend was as full of stories as ever, and visiting hour passed all too quickly.

Nichole was even more excited by Mrs. Bandler's descriptions of Red Cross nursing than Shelley and Bernie

29

had been. "Oh," she kept saying, clasping her hands, her eyes sparkling as the old woman talked. "It's all too wonderful! It's too, too thrilling!"

Mrs. Bandler couldn't help laughing. "If I'd known my life was going to be so interesting, I would have taken notes."

"If I'd known World War Two was this exciting," Nichole told her, "I'd have read Mr. Haggerty's history assignment."

"And if I'd known you four were having such a good time in here, I'd have joined you," the floor nurse said kindly. "I'm sorry to do this, but visiting hours are now officially over."

Mrs. Bandler stiffened and folded her arms. "Run along, girls," she said. "Don't make the nurse's job harder than it already is."

"We'll be back again soon," Shelley promised.

"We sure will," agreed Bernie.

"I can't wait to hear the next installment," Nichole said.

"Well, I hope I don't get well too quickly," Mrs. Bandler told them, waving from her bed. "Because, frankly, I can't wait to tell it."

As the three girls walked off with the floor nurse, Bernie thought about what Mrs. Bandler had said about getting well. "I know we're not supposed to discuss patients' conditions with them," she asked the nurse, "but can you tell us what's wrong with Mrs. Bandler?"

Even though she was off duty, Bernie could hardly resist ducking into each room they passed to check on water pitchers or to see if anyone needed something. "I'm not sure there's anything *medical* wrong with Mrs. Bandler," the nurse told them as they continued down the hall.

"The nursing home sent her here because she broke her hip. She should have been discharged by now, but she keeps getting infections and colds and she doesn't get any better.'' She stopped at the reception desk, picked up a clipboard, then walked with the girls to the elevator. ''We've checked her for anemia. Her blood and heart are fine. Personally,'' she said, as a bell rang and an elevator door slid open, ''I think she's just lost the will to live since her husband died.''

''Her husband?'' Nichole held the elevator open, but the girls didn't get on.

''Yes,'' the nurse explained. ''When we checked with the home about family, they said her husband was the only family member. And that when he died last year, she went into a severe depression. She couldn't even take care of herself. That's how she ended up in the nursing home.'' She shook her head. ''Sometimes I think loneliness is the worst disease of all.''

''I have to be the luckiest guy in Ridge Dale,'' Roger announced on Saturday night. ''Correction,'' he added, smiling at Bernie, Nichole, and Shelley. ''Make that the luckiest guy in the whole state of New Jersey. Friends like you and a party like this sure make me feel stupid for complaining about a little thing like a broken arm!'' He looked happily around the crowded recreation room in the O'Connors' basement. ''Thanks, everyone.''

The group of boys and girls pressed in around him, lots of them shaking his ''new'' right hand. Bernie and Shelley and Nichole had invited all the regular gang, even some of their friends from Mercy. ''My man,'' Blake Willard said, pumping Roger's arm up and down vigorously. ''I figure if I shake your hand hard enough, I can prevent some of your great passes against us next season.''

''Not a chance, Blake,'' Roger laughed. ''I intend to get in shape and stay in shape.''

''Glad you've gotten off that cast,'' Clifford Foster told

him shyly. "It must be pretty rough being a one-armed man."

"You bet it is!" Roger slapped the slim boy on the back. "It feels so great to have both arms back, I could hug everyone. How about it, Cliff?" He opened his arms wide, and Cliff ducked away, embarrassed.

"If he doesn't want a hug, I sure do," Elise Sheridan exclaimed. A roly-poly girl who'd clearly eaten too many of the doughnuts her father made in his famous bakery, Elise encircled the handsome football player with her own chubby arms.

"My turn," insisted Beverly Feldon, a Ridge Dale majorette. One of the girls' good friends, she was a bubbly, friendly dynamo who was into more school activities and clubs than she could count. She, too, gave Roger a big hug. So did Shelley and Nichole and Bernie. Bernie felt her cheeks redden as Roger whispered in her ear, "I saved the best for last."

Now Shelley scanned the faces in the crowd. "Where's Mr. Music?" she asked.

"Here I am!" Struggling to the front of the room, Teddy carried two speakers and a huge case of CDs with him. He had the biggest collection in school, and no party was complete without him. "What'll it be, Honored Guest?" he asked Roger. "Heavy metal, industrial, rap, blues, or rock?"

"I think we should let our hostess decide," Roger said, smiling at Bernie. "After all, if she and her folks are crazy enough to allow a bunch like us into their home, she should be able to choose what music we shake the rafters to!"

"Anything loud," Bernie decided. "My dad said as long as he hears music, he won't come down to check on us." Everyone laughed, and as Teddy put on the first album, they cleared a space in the middle of the floor.

Around the edges of the room, people gossiped and ate and drank, while in the center, they danced in two's and three's. Some did the latest crazes, moving their bodies in smooth, skillful gyrations; others, less sure of themselves, danced quietly on the sidelines; while still others preferred to watch, tapping their feet to the beat.

"Boy," Bev Feldon told Bernie, dunking a chip into Shelley's special sour cream dip, "this is the first big party of the year." She pulled a soda can from the garbage can Bernie's father had filled with ice. "And I only have one question: How are they going to get any better?"

Bernie laughed. "Well, for one thing," she said, pointing to the center of the room, "Teddy could learn to dance." Sure enough, Teddy was moving through the middle of the crowd on the makeshift dance floor. In fact, it looked as if there were lots of Teddies, each one wiggling and spinning and sweating. The gangly comic was everywhere, dancing with so many girls at once that most of the other boys were forced to stand and watch. He even raced over to the refreshment table, grabbed Bev, and pulled her, laughing, onto the floor. Holding his stomach, unbuttoning his shirt, spinning on the seat of his jeans, Teddy was, as always, the center of attention.

"My pal Teddy sure knows how to have a good time." Roger joined Bernie, watching his friend tear wildly around the room.

"He sure does," agreed Bernie. "I wish I could let go like that." Bernie sighed.

"Let go of what?" asked Roger, studying her face. "Is something wrong?"

Bernie felt guilty about talking shop. "It's nothing," she told him. "Just hospital stuff." She couldn't help thinking about Mrs. Bandler. About an old woman sitting alone while so many people in this room were having a good time.

"Hey," Roger reminded her. "That hospital stuff is going to be something we're going to share starting next week. Didn't Blake tell you he dragged me in to sign up after school yesterday?"

"He did?" Good old Blake, Bernie thought. That charmer could certainly accomplish miracles.

"Yep. I start on Tuesday. With you."

Bernie felt a little uneasy. "With me?" she asked.

"Sure." Roger grinned happily. "I'm going to make sure our schedules match."

"That's great." Bernie hoped it would be. She remembered Roger stopping to wave at her during a time out, and the awful thud as he'd hit the ground.

"Now, what's your problem at Mercy?" Roger leaned forward, ready to listen.

Bernie told him about the mysterious Mrs. Nobody, about how she had once been an active, busy nurse and how she needed to be needed again.

"I sure know how it feels to be sidelined," Roger told her. "Don't worry, Dr. Thornton's on the case now." Smiling with new confidence, he leaned back against the card table where the girls had set the chips and pretzels. "That nice old woman is in the best of hands." Instead of connecting with the table, though, Roger's elbow had landed in a bowl of dip. Thrown off balance, he fell into the table. In turn, the table collapsed and all the bowls skidded across its face and shattered on the floor.

As she looked down at her fallen friend, surrounded by mounds of sour cream and heaps of chips, Bernie had to laugh. "Well, you may not have the best hands," she said, helping him to his feet. "But at least your heart's in the right place!"

4

Dr. Thornton Reporting for Duty

"Honestly, sometimes I think I'm crazy." Bev Feldon shook her head. "I've got three different club meetings all at the same time after school today." She took a bite of the cafeteria special, a chili burger.

"Why don't you just skip two of the meetings?" Shelley, seated next to Bev, dug into her own burger. "Will anybody really miss you?"

Bev considered the suggestion. "I'm afraid so," she told Shelley. "I'm the president of all three clubs."

Bernie and Nichole, seated across from Bev and Shelley, laughed. "You are too much, Beverly Feldon!" Bernie scolded. "Can't you ever do anything halfway?"

Their friend ran her fingers through her short, dark hair. "Well, let's see," she said. "I could never, ever give up twirling for the band . . ."

"Of course not," Nichole agreed. "That little blue and

white miniskirt you wear is just too adorable." She placed a napkin carefully over the lap of her own brand new suede skirt. "Why don't you give up something you don't get to dress up for?"

Bev giggled. "That would be everything else," she said. "But I couldn't let the Service Club down. We're just getting that day-care program started." She ticked off all her activities on the fingers of her hands. "Then there's the Spanish Club, we have our banquet coming up . . ."

"Am I invited, Señorita?" asked Teddy, putting his tray down next to her. "I don't speak Spanish, but I'm an expert eater."

"Well, you'd better be the best eater in the world," Shelley told him, pushing her tray away. "Because today's special is possibly the world's worst." She made a face as if she'd just eaten a plateful of lemons.

"No prob." Teddy grabbed a bottle of catsup from the center of the table. "In a little less than three months of dining at Chez Ridge Dale, I have perfected the secret of making anything go down easy." Grinning, he proceeded to pour almost the entire bottle of catsup over his chili burger, then bit into the sloppy mess. "Mmmmm!" he said. "I hardly taste a thing!"

As the others reached for the catsup bottle, Roger arrived with his tray. "Hey, there," he said, cheerfully. "What's up?"

"Hi, Rog," Bernie said. "We're testing Teddy's cafeteria formula: Ridge Dale food plus infinite catsup equals something you can swallow."

Roger laughed. "Well, I think I'll stick to my own formula," he told them. "Eat and run. I've hardly got time to eat at all. I forgot I have a biology quiz next period."

"The Science Club!" Bev interrupted. "That's one I almost forgot about. But I'm only vice president."

36

Roger and Teddy looked puzzled.

"We're trying to help Bev sort out her social life," Shelley explained. "It seems Miss Into Everything has gotten herself into hot water."

"I really do have to cut back," Bev conceded. "I just don't know which activity to give up." She paused, remembering what had happened in U.S. history that morning. "Although it looks like there's at least one club that's not going to need me anymore."

"What do you mean?" asked Nichole.

"Mr. Haggerty told us in class today that if there's not more interest in the History Club, the school's going to eliminate it." She sighed with relief. "And since I'm vice president and program director, I guess that helps solve my problem."

"Maybe not," Shelley told her. "Maybe it's going to make you busier than ever, Bev." Shelley was smiling broadly.

"How?"

Shelley looked across the table at Nichole. "Nick," she asked, "remember how bored you've been with your history reading assignments?"

Nichole tossed her blond hair. "They go on forever," she complained. "Simply forever!"

Now Shelley folded her arms on the table and asked, "And do you remember how bored you were when Mrs. Bandler talked about the same period in history you've been reading about?"

Nichole's blue eyes widened. "Bored?" she asked indignantly. "I was most certainly *not* bored." She remembered the wonderful, romantic stories the old woman had told. "I was thrilled. Why, I was on the edge of my seat the whole time!"

"Exactly!" said Shelley. She looked at her friends triumphantly.

Everyone looked confused. Everyone except Bernie. "Oh, Shell. You're a genius. You're a terrific, wonderful whiz!"

"What on earth are you two talking about?" asked Bev.

"Have we got a club program for you!" Bernie told her. "Right, Shell?"

"You are going to save the History Club," Shelley promised. "And you just may give a wonderful old lady a reason to live, too!" Full of excitement, Bernie and Shelley and Nichole described Mrs. Bandler to Bev: how she made World War Two come alive just by telling about her life; how she was too clever and lively to spend her days in a nursing home; how she needed something to do.

"And you think she'd talk to the History Club?" asked Bev.

"We won't know until we ask her," said Bernie.

"I'll visit her when I work in the flower room at Mercy on Monday!" said Nichole.

"Great!" decided Bev. "I'll talk to Mr. Haggerty this afternoon." But as lunch period ended and the bell sounded, she looked frustrated. "Wait a minute," she said. "If Mr. Haggerty likes this idea, he'll ask Mrs. Bandler to talk to the club." She walked with her friends toward the back of the room, then placed her tray on the conveyor belt into the kitchen. "And if the kids like her as much as you three did, the club will get bigger."

"That's the idea!" Bernie told her happily.

But Bev was far from happy. "And if the club gets bigger, I'll still be vice president," she reasoned. "They may even elect me president, and I'll be busier than ever." She turned to the group as everyone burst out laughing. "Thanks a lot. Some friends you are!"

Roger looked just as terrific in his maroon volunteer's blazer as Bernie had known he would. But he was even more nervous than she'd expected. "Relax, Rog," she told him, as he walked with her and Shelley up the front steps of Mercy Hospital on Tuesday after school. "This is just beginner's shakes. You'll do fine."

Roger wasn't so sure. "I feel clammy all over," he told his friends. He paused on the stone stairs, one arm leaning on the railing. "What if I find out I can't stand the sight of blood?"

Shelley stopped on the bottom step. Her dark braid was wrapped neatly into a knot on the top of her head, and her striped uniform was freshly cleaned and pressed. "Do you mean to tell me, Ace Athlete," she said, an expression of disbelief on her face, "that with all the sports you've played, you've never seen blood?"

"Only my own." Roger smiled sheepishly. "I've seen lots of that with all the spills I've taken." He shook his head. "But what if I can't watch other people bleed? What if I get sick?"

"Hey," Bernie told him, touching his arm gently, "don't worry so much. We all felt the same way." As she looked up the stairs toward the hospital entrance, with its magnificent carving of a lion and a lamb above the door, she remembered her first day at Mercy. How impressed she'd been walking through that doorway, how full of nervous energy and excitement! "Besides," she added, "you'll be in training this week, so Mrs. Hurley will be right beside you all the time."

"I just wish you two were training with me," he said, turning and walking up the last few steps. "I sure could use some expert advice."

Bernie and Shelley exchanged looks. Had they really been *this* nervous? "You'll have all the expert advice you need," Shelley assured him. "In fact, you'll learn so much it'll make you dizzy." She remembered how confused she'd been trying to memorize all the different units in the

39

four wings of the hospital, how she'd worried about forgetting where Central Supplies was or what the abbreviations on patient diet lists meant.

"I promise," Bernie told him as the three of them walked inside and headed toward the Volunteer Office, "everything will be great." As she and Shelley signed in, she hoped it was true. She looked up with relief as Mrs. Hurley walked in. "Maybe we'll see you on duty," she told Roger. "Good luck!"

"He won't need luck," Pat Hurley said, as she took her newest volunteer by the arm and led him to the elevators in the hall. "He's got strong arms and a broad back. We can use both around here." She waved. "Good luck, yourselves."

The girls waved back, then checked their assignments on the duty roster. "Great!" Shelley hugged Bernie when she saw the list. "We're both on Long Term Care!"

Bernie's green eyes sparkled. "That means we can visit with Mrs. Bandler early," she said. She looked serious. "And it also means I won't have time to worry about a certain new volunteer."

"Roger will do just fine," Shelley told her, as they headed for the elevators, too.

"I sure hope so," Bernie said uncertainly. But before she had time to let her little doubts grow into big worries, the elevator doors slid open to the third floor reception desk and the floor nurse handed them the diet lists for the unit. "Hello, you two," she said, smiling. "Welcome back."

"Thanks," said Bernie. "How's Mrs. Bandler?"

"Well," admitted the nurse. "She could be better." She rose to her feet as a patient call button lit up on the monitor behind the desk. "She was doing fine until a friend of yours, another volunteer, visited yesterday."

"Nichole!" Shelley couldn't understand. "But Nichole

had good news for Mrs. Bandler. It should have made her better, not worse."

The nurse started down the hall. "After you've done the water carafes, why don't you check on her?" she suggested, turning back to them for a minute. "I think she could use some cheering up."

Worried, Shelley and Bernie rushed off to get the water cart and fill a pitcher of water for each room. Carefully, they checked the diet list to make sure they didn't give a pitcher to any patient whose name was marked "NPO." The letters stood for a Latin phrase that meant "nothing by mouth," and the girls knew it usually meant a patient was on intravenous feeding, and it could be dangerous to let him or her drink anything at all.

They had worked their way around the whole unit, delivering fresh water pitchers and clean towels to all the rooms except for Mrs. Bandler's, when they heard the commotion down the hall.

Looking behind them, Bernie and Shelley saw a group of nurses and several patients gathered outside the door to one of the empty rooms they had passed earlier. Curious, the two girls retraced their steps and joined the group, who were whispering and laughing as they watched what was happening in the room. "What is it?" asked Bernie as they neared the crowd.

"It's a training class," a nurse told them. She was peering over the shoulders of a burly orderly who blocked her view. "And it's a doozy," she laughed. "Nurse Francis must have made that boy take that bed apart thirty times already."

"Forty is more like it," the orderly laughed and turned around to face them. "I've never seen anyone so slow to catch on to bedmaking. If that kid's face gets any redder, they could use it to read by!"

With a sinking feeling, Bernie looked past the orderly

into the room. Sure enough, it was a training class. Five volunteers in training stood around a bed while each took turns making it. Mrs. Hurley watched while one of the nurses gave a demonstration, then stepped aside to let a handsome, very embarrassed boy try again. It was Roger.

Shelley and Bernie watched as he fumbled with the sheets, trying to tuck them in, trying to leave them as smooth as the nurse had. The other volunteers waited, tired and impatient, while he pulled and tugged and left the bed looking as though someone had waged a battle on it. "No, I'm afraid that's still not right," the nurse said, sounding tired herself.

Roger hung his head. "But I did just what you said," he insisted.

"No," the nurse told him. "Remember I said the seam side of the bottom sheet faces the bed." She sighed and tore the sheets off the bed. "Let's try it again."

Shelley turned away, embarrassed for Roger. "Gee," she said. "Why don't they let him off the hook?"

One of the nurses heard her. "Hey, you know darn well why they don't," she told Shelley. "A little thing like the right side of the sheet can make a big difference, especially to an elderly patient." She shook her head. "I worked in a nursing home where they didn't care which side of the sheet ended up against the patient's skin. You should have seen the bedsores some of those old folks got!"

"Poor guy," the orderly sympathized. "He's been sweating over that bed for twenty minutes now. Maybe he just ought to give up."

"No!" Bernie heard herself saying. "He's going to learn. He's going to be a great volunteer." She strode off down the hall, tears of frustration in her eyes. When Shelley caught up with her, she turned to her friend. "Oh, Shell," she said, "I was afraid this would happen. I should

42

have never asked Roger to try Mercy. What if he can't make it, after all?"

"Don't be silly," Shelley told her. "We all made mistakes at first. Remember how much trouble we had folding wheelchairs?"

Bernie knew Shelley was right. "And how about that time I delivered flowers to all the wrong patients?" she asked. She could still see the surprised faces on the patients who had to give their beautiful arrangements back. "I guess it just takes time."

"Sure," said Shelley. "Now, in case you've forgotten, we have one last pitcher of water to replace. In room 308."

"Mrs. Bandler!" said Bernie. "I almost forgot." Grabbing the pitcher from the cart, she walked to 308. "Hi," she ventured, walking quietly toward Mrs. Bandler's bed. "Can we come in?"

The old woman was sitting up, facing the window. She looked almost as sad and lonely as she had the first day they'd visited. But when she turned toward them, she wore a little smile. "Oh, hello," she said. "It certainly is good to see you."

"Did Nichole tell you about your command performance?" Shelley asked. "We're so excited that you might talk to our History Club!"

The two girls were so pleased with their good news, they hardly gave Mrs. Bandler a chance to talk. "We have a friend who's the program director for the club," Shelley bubbled. "She says Mr. Haggerty, our history teacher, is thrilled. He told her the club is so small right now that they could probably all come visit you right here in the hospital if you can't travel to the school."

"That's nice, dear," Mrs. Bandler began. "But . . ."

"And later, when you're feeling stronger," Bernie promised, "we could hold meetings at the nursing home.

43

Mr. Haggerty says there must be lots of residents who could make history come alive.''

"Well, I'm sure there are," Mrs. Bandler told them. "But I'm not one of them."

"Why not?" Shelley asked. "You'd be an awesome teacher, Mrs. B!"

"I don't think so," Mrs. Bandler said. "I don't think that's a very good idea at all."

"Why on earth not?" Shelley was upset. She couldn't understand why Mrs. Bandler was spoiling all their terrific plans. But Bernie saw the frightened look in the old woman's eyes. It looked very familiar. "What's wrong, Mrs. Bandler?" she asked gently. "Why don't you want to speak to the kids?"

Mrs. Bandler folded her small, delicate hands in her lap. "Oh, it's not that I don't want to, Bernadette," she said. "It's just that I'm, well, you know . . ."

Bernie recognized Mrs. Bandler's frightened expression. She had seen it just a few minutes ago on Roger. "You're afraid," she said softly. "You've got the beginner's shakes."

"I love talking to you girls," Mrs. Bandler confessed. "It's just that I would never be able to talk to a room full of strangers."

"Not even if it would save the History Club?" asked Bernie.

"What do you mean, dear?"

Shelley sat down in the chair by Mrs. Bandler's bed. "She means no one in school cares about history," she explained. "Only three or four people show up for the club meetings."

"Not care about history?" asked Mrs. Bandler. "Why, that's like saying nothing exciting ever happened in the past." She leaned forward in the bed and shrugged her shoulders. "In fact, it's like saying nothing exciting ever

44

happens at all." She looked at the girls. "Because what's happening today is going to be history tomorrow."

"Mr. Haggerty loves his subject," Bernie told their new friend. "But he just doesn't know how to make it interesting. He doesn't have your knack for making everything come to life."

"Knack?" Mrs. Bandler looked surprised.

"Of course," Bernie told her. "Don't you know what fun you are to talk to? Didn't you see the way Nichole hung on every word you said?"

"Well, she did seem to like my stories."

"And those stories were about the same period in history that she's supposed to be studying in school," Shelley said.

"She's *supposed* to be studying World War Two," Bernie added. "But she's not. Because she's bored."

Shelley saw the way Harriet Bandler's face had begun to light up, the enthusiasm behind her shy smile. "Didn't you say you wanted to be useful, Mrs. Bandler? Wouldn't helping a whole class of kids care about the past be useful?"

"I hadn't thought of it that way." Mrs. Bandler leaned back in her bed. "You know, I have lots of old clippings and photos from the war years. Maybe the students would be interested in them."

Bernie was thrilled. "Maybe?" she said, clapping her hands. "There's no maybe about it, Mrs. B." She leaned across the bed to hug the old woman. "You are going to be the best history teacher Ridge Dale ever had!"

All three were smiling when the girls said good-bye and started back to the reception desk. "Well, at least one thing's gone right today," said Bernie with relief. "I can't wait to tell Bev the Club can visit next week!"

"She sure looked happy, didn't she?" asked Shelley. "That's one school function I don't want to miss."

45

The two girls were chatting happily when they noticed that the training class was clustered in the hall ahead of them. Everyone had finally ''graduated'' bed-making it seemed, because now the boys and girls were working with wheelchairs. Bernie could see Mrs. Hurley demonstrating how to brake a chair and how to raise the foot rest for a patient. ''I'm glad Roger didn't notice us eavesdropping on his bed-making lesson,'' she whispered to Shelley.

''And I hope he does better now,'' her friend added, smiling as they neared the group of new volunteers. ''Hi, Mrs. Hurley,'' she said. ''Hi, everyone.''

The Volunteer Director and her class looked up. ''Hello, Shelley,'' Mrs. Hurley said. ''Hello, Bernie.''

At the sound of her name, the sandy-haired boy who'd been pushing the wheelchair turned around. It was Roger. Seeing Bernie, he smiled and let go of the wheelchair to wave at her.

Because the corridor ran slightly downhill, the wheelchair kept going even though Roger had stopped. Rolling down the hall, the empty chair sailed into the big orderly who'd been watching Roger make beds. Now, though, he was pushing a cart filled with meal trays for dinner.

As the chair left his grasp, Roger's mouth opened, but no sound came out. With his back to the teens, the orderly never saw the wheelchair come rolling toward him. When it hit him, the meal cart went flying, and so did the man himself. Unable to stop himself, he fell into a nurse who was standing in the hall with a clipboard. When the big man barreled into her, the nurse dropped her clipboard, which clattered to the floor and landed at Mrs. Hurley's feet.

Bernie and Shelley could hardly believe their eyes. The orderly lay on his side, and the whole hall was filled with a trail of spilled food and broken glass. Mr. Klutz had really done it this time! And this time, it wasn't Roger who'd taken a tumble. It had been an orderly with dinner trays. And dinner was definitely going to be late!

Roger stared dumbfounded at the results of his accident, the shiny bits of shattered glass, the mounds of mashed potatoes and Jell-O, the damp gravy stains spreading across the floor. Finally, he stooped to help the orderly to his feet, then looked apologetically at Mrs. Hurley.

Bernie held her breath as she watched the Volunteer Director survey the littered hall, turn on her heel, and head for the supply closet. The boys and girls stood, shocked and silent, in the middle of the hall until she returned.

"Let's get busy and clean this up," Mrs. Hurley said when she reappeared. After she had handed brooms and towels out to the class, she looked at Roger. Blushing more than ever, he was on his hands and knees, mopping up the mess. "As for you, young man," she told him in a harsh voice that didn't sound at all like the calm, cheerful woman they knew, "I want to see you in my office right away."

5

Code 9!

Bernie and Shelley had never seen Roger look so discouraged. "I'm a total failure," he told them when he met them outside Mrs. Hurley's office. "I'm good for nothing. My life is ruined!"

The two girls jumped up from the plastic chairs in which they'd been waiting. "What did she say?" asked Bernie. "You were in there forever!"

Roger worked his long arms out of the maroon blazer and slung it over his shoulder. Then he headed toward the exit. His steps were slow and heavy, like an old man's. "She said I'm on probation." Standing to one side as the big glass doors swung open, he let Bernie and Shelley walk through in front of him. "She said Mercy might not be able to afford my help."

Shelley looked hurriedly at Bernie. "Probation?" she asked. "What does that mean?"

Bernie sounded relieved. "It means she's giving him a second chance," she said. She turned to Roger, picturing the disaster her friend had just caused on the third floor. "Everybody's entitled to one mistake, Rog."

"Sure," said Shelley, trying to help. "Yours was just bigger than most, that's all." As soon as she'd said it, she was sorry. She covered her mouth, wishing she could take the words back.

"Big?" said Roger. "That mess upstairs wasn't just big, Shelley. It was colossal. It was . . . it was . . ."

"Funny?" suggested Bernie. She remembered the way the empty wheelchair and the heavy orderly and the nurse had flipped over like dominoes, and the way the clipboard had clattered across the floor.

"It looked just like a ghost was riding that wheelchair down the hall," Shelley said, starting to giggle. "The case of the invisible patient!"

Bernie laughed, too, but Roger shook his head. "This is serious," he told them. "What if there had been a patient in that chair? What if I never learn to make a bed? What if Mrs. Hurley's right, and I end up hurting more than I help?"

The three friends were crossing Dale Avenue, and Shelley decided this wasn't the best time to leave Roger alone. "Before you go home, Rog, why don't we talk things over?" She pointed to Pizza Paradise. "I'll bet some of the gang's digging into a Deluxe pie right now."

Roger looked at the pizzeria, the familiar sign painted with clouds and a winged pizza slice. "No, thanks," he said. "I don't feel much like company."

Bernie hated to see him so depressed. "But, Roger," she told him, "don't you see?" She grabbed his arm. "Mrs. Hurley wouldn't have given you another chance if she didn't think you could make it. She wouldn't . . ."

"Thanks," Roger said. "I know what you two are trying to do." He took his blazer and handed it to Bernie. "Here, give this to Mrs. Hurley when you go in on Thursday. Tell her she won't have to worry about mistake number two."

"Roger!" Bernie stared at the crumpled coat in her arms. "You mean you're quitting?"

"I mean I'm saving Mercy the trouble of kicking me out." He turned and headed down the street. "I wouldn't have made it anyway."

"Roger, wait." Bernie ran after him.

"Look, Bern," he told her quietly. "I'd really rather be by myself. See you guys in school tomorrow. Okay?" He waited until Bernie rejoined Shelley, then waved to them both and headed home without looking back.

Mathew had been put to bed, but Bernie's younger sisters were still up when she got home. "Tell us about the hospital!" Sara begged. She and Tracy ran to meet their big sister at the door. Behind them trailed little Kelly, her favorite doll in her arms. "Did you save any lives?" she asked.

Bernie laughed, then studied Kelly's doll. Its head was wrapped in a white towel, from which strands of yellow hair peeked. "What have you done to poor Matilda?" she asked.

Kelly looked down at Matilda, then up at Bernie. "Matilda hurt herself," she said solemnly. "So I had to take her to the hospital."

Bernie folded her arms. She knew how much her youngest sister loved to pretend. "And just where is this hospital?" she asked.

"I'm afraid it was in the middle of the kitchen table." Mrs. O'Connor, smiling broadly, joined them. "We performed a heroic, lifesaving operation with the potato peeler and a pair of scissors." She watched as Kelly hugged her doll tightly. "The patient is resting comfortably." She turned and headed back toward the kitchen. "What do you

50

say we all celebrate with some apple cobbler while it's still warm?''

"Mmmmm!'' Bernie loved the way her mother mixed cinnamon and sugary apples, then baked them under a crisp pastry crust. All four girls followed Mrs. O'Connor into the kitchen, and helped themselves to steaming plates of the delicious, gooey treat.

"The nurse made Matilda all better," Kelly explained, as she propped her doll into the chair beside her. "Just like you do at Mercy, Bern.''

Bernie grinned. "Hey," she said, tousling her sister's dark curls. "How many times do I have to tell you, Kiddo? I'm not a nurse. I'm just a JV.''

"Just nothing,'' her mother told her. "You know how much the nurses count on volunteers." She handed her eldest a heaping plate of cobbler. "You make it a lot easier for them to do their jobs.''

"We're supposed to, Mom," Bernie said. All of a sudden, in the middle of the delicious, warm smell and the fun at the table, she remembered Roger. "But it looks like some JVs are giving Mercy nothing but trouble!''

Mary O'Connor noticed the way Bernie only picked at her favorite dessert. "What do you mean, Honey?" she asked.

"Today was Roger's first day of training," Bernie told her mother. She paused, remembering the way Roger had left her and Shelley to walk home alone. "And it may be his last.''

"I don't think boys should be nurses," Tracy pronounced, finishing her cobbler and reaching for the milk carton Mrs. O'Connor had placed on the table.

"Yeah," Sara agreed readily. "Boys are dumb.''

Mrs. O'Connor smiled. "Ladies, she said, "may I remind you that we have two—er, 'boys' in our family, and neither one strikes me as dumb.''

"She means Dad and Matt," Tracy explained to Kelly. "But they don't really count."

Bernie pushed her plate away. "First of all," she said, "it's not fair that Dad's not here to defend his honor." She poured a glass of milk for Kelly. "And second of all, there are plenty of boys—I mean, men—who are nurses, real nurses. At Mercy and lots of other hospitals, too."

"And third of all," Mrs. O'Connor announced, "it's time for three future nurses to go to bed." She winked at Bernie. "I think your sister and I have something to discuss."

"Mom!" insisted Tracy. "I'm in the fifth grade." she looked pleadingly at her mother. "I'm older than Sara and Kelly, and I should get to stay up later."

"Yeah," added Sara. "I'm in second grade, so I should stay up later than Kelly." She pointed to her little sister. "She's in no grade at all."

Kelly put down her fork and stood up from her chair, knocking poor Matilda on the floor. "Kindergarten is too a grade," she said.

"You're all right," their mother replied calmly. "Tracy, you get to read in your bed because you're the oldest." She watched as Tracy put her plate in the sink and left the room, smiling proudly.

"And Sara, you get to tell Kelly a good-night story because you know so many good ones." Sara, thrilled at her assignment, took her little sister by the hand and headed up the stairs behind Tracy. But Kelly pulled back, anxious to hear more. "What do *I* get to do, Mommy?" she asked.

Mrs. O'Connor stopped to think. But Bernie thought faster. She scooped Kelly up in her arms and whirled her around the room. "You get to tell me how to spell your name, because kindergartners are so smart!" she said.

Kelly giggled. "K," she said when Bernie put her

52

down. "E," she recited next, her face stiff with concentration. "L and another L," she said, one finger in her mouth. "And . . ." She paused, trying to remember. "And . . ." She looked around the room.

"I'll bet you can remember if we all say it together," Bernie suggested. "K," she began, and her mother and sisters joined in. "E," they all said together. "L, L, Y."

"Y! Y! It's Y!" Kelly sang out. "I remembered!" Happily, she gathered up her doll, and took Sara's hand. "Come on," she urged, scampering up the stairs. "I want to hear about Sleeping Beauty."

When the kitchen had quieted, Mrs. O'Connor pulled her chair closer to the table and put her arm on Bernie's. "Now, Honey, let's talk."

Bernie sighed. It was a relief to be able to sort the day out. She told her mother about Roger's accident and his probation. She described how embarrassed he'd been, and how he'd given his jacket to her to take back to Mercy. "I think he means it, Mom," she said. "I think he's giving up."

"Would that be so terrible?" asked her mother. "You know I gave up something everybody thought I should do, and I've never been sorry." Mrs. O'Connor had been a bank vice president before her children were born. But she always said the decision to give up her career had been easy. She loved being a full-time mother, and she thought it was much more important than worrying about how other people spent their money!

"It's different with Roger, Mom," Bernie explained. "He can't play football right now, and there isn't anything else he wants to do." She stood up and took the milk carton to the refrigerator. "Besides, he doesn't even know whether he could be a good volunteer or not. He's quitting before he gives it a fair try."

"It's pretty rough to be embarrassed like that in public,'' Mrs. O'Connor said. ''But if he really wants to help, Roger may reconsider.'' She walked to the sink and let the water run over the dishes the girls had piled there. ''After all, he's got a pretty good friend who believes in him.''

Bernie closed the refrigerator and turned to face her mother. ''That's just it, Mom,'' she said. ''I'm not sure I *do* believe in Rog.'' She sank back into a chair at the table. ''Oh, I think he's gentle and smart and just about the cutest boy around.'' She sighed. ''But I'm not sure he's right for Mercy. I *want* him to be, but I'm just not sure.''

''The wanting part is what counts, Honey,'' Bernie's mother said, kissing her on the forehead. ''Just be patient and let Roger work things out. You said yourself, he's a smart boy.''

After they'd turned out the kitchen lights and gone upstairs, Bernie lay awake in her bed. Her glow-in-the-dark stars twinkled cheerfully overhead, but instead of soothing her to sleep, they made her toss and turn. Each time she shut her eyes, she felt them sparkling behind her lids. And when she opened her eyes, there they were, shining like the tiny fragments of glass Roger's accident had scattered across the hospital floor.

''Well?'' Nichole raced up to Bernie after lunch on Thursday. ''Did you get him to change his mind?'' She and Shelley had left Bernie alone with Roger, hoping a miracle would happen and Roger would decide to come with them to Mercy after school.

Bernie shrugged. ''I tried everything,'' she said. ''I even told him about the time my dad was trying to improve my backhand, and I swung too far and broke his glasses!''

''You did?'' Shelley laughed. ''What did your dad do?''

''Bought a new pair of glasses.'' Bernie's smile faded.

54

"Roger says that's nothing compared to his accident. He says he's afraid the next time will be worse. He doesn't want to go on with the training."

"Gee," said Nichole. "When you two told me about the trouble he got into, it sounded kind of funny, sort of like a sitcom on TV." She had loved their description of the chain reaction pileup in the hallway. "But this is no joking matter." She paused, remembering her own training. "I mean, I know what it's like to feel you'll never make it."

"But you *did* make it, Nick," Bernie told her. "Even though you got down on yourself, you didn't give up." She sighed. "Maybe he just doesn't want it enough."

Nichole's blue eyes looked stern. She folded her arms across the front of her striped tunic. "Now don't you go giving up on him, too," she said. "What kind of friends would we be if we let him pass up the chance to find out what he can do?" She took her two friends by the arms. "Let's go see Mrs. Hurley this afternoon," she suggested. "We can ask her to give him a few more days to come to his senses."

Bernie hugged Nichole. For days and weeks, her flighty friend would think about nothing but boys and clothes. And then all of a sudden, like right now, she'd show how kindhearted she really was! "You're right, Nick," she said. "You are absolutely right. If anyone deserves a second chance, it's Rog. And we're going to make sure he gets it." She bit her lip, and added, "Even if he doesn't know he wants it."

The girls had agreed to meet by the stone bench in front of Ridge Dale's gym right after school. But neither Shelley nor Bernie was surprised when Nichole was late. "She's probably in the girls' room," Shelley guessed, "checking her lipstick in the mirror."

55

"For a girl who's picture pretty anyway," Bernie said, "Nick sure does spend a lot of time in front of the mirror."

"Not this time, though," observed Shelley, looking up at a lone figure who raced to join them. As she got closer, the girls could see that Nichole certainly hadn't been near a mirror. She had no lipstick on, and a long strand of golden hair had escaped from the neat knot on top of her head.

"That boy's impossible!" she said, as she caught up to her two friends and the three of them hurried down Dale Avenue toward the hospital. "He listens about as well as a stone wall!"

Bernie knew what had happened. She looked at the red blazer she carried folded over her left arm. "Let me guess, Nick," she said. "You tried to talk Roger into coming, didn't you?"

"It's just that I love Mercy," Nichole confessed. "And I'm sure Roger would, too, if he gave it a chance." She tucked her stray hair into the knot. "Besides," she added, "the way he's moping around is enough to make you cry."

Bernie nodded. "I know," she said. "Which is why we've got to hurry and get to Mercy early. If Mrs. Hurley's willing to let him come back, maybe we can still change his mind."

The girls quickened their pace, and reached the Volunteer Office with five minutes to spare. "You go," Shelley told Bernie. "You always know what to say."

"Not this time," Bernie said. "I don't even know how to start."

"Why don't you start by telling me where your friend Roger is?" Mrs. Hurley, looking as warm and cheery as ever, surprised them by walking into the office behind them. "I've just been setting up a special safety lesson for our training class. I think he'll learn a lot."

"I'm sure he would if he were here," Bernie told her. "But . . . he . . . that is, he decided . . ."

Mrs. Hurley saw the embarrassed look on Bernie's face. Then she saw the maroon blazer she was carrying. "You mean he's decided not to complete the training," she finished for the stammering girl.

"Yes," Bernie admitted quietly. "He felt so awful about what happened."

"And I'm afraid I didn't help matters," the Volunteer Director offered. "I guess I was a little hard on him."

"I think he's been harder on himself," Nichole told them. "He feels totally rotten, Mrs. Hurley."

"Well, I hope you'll tell him we strongly disagree," Mrs. Hurley said. She smiled, putting an arm on Nichole's shoulder. "And I also hope you'll tell him that it's not too late to change his mind. Training doesn't end until this weekend, you know."

The girls smiled with relief. "Thanks, thanks so much," Bernie told her. She folded Roger's blazer and laid it in the locker the JVs used for their coats and purses. "If you don't mind," she told Mrs. Hurley, "I'll keep this for a while. I think Roger just needs a chance to think things over."

"Fine," Mrs. Hurley agreed. "Meanwhile, you've got a chance to give out dinner menus on Orthopedics."

Grateful, the three JVs signed the duty roster and went to work. Bernie was glad to have so much to do. It took her mind off Roger and put it on helping Ortho patients with arms and legs in casts write out their menu orders. Then, when the meal trays came up from the cafeteria, she and Shelley and Nichole fed the patients who couldn't eat by themselves.

After they had cleaned up the dinner trays and stacked them in the unit's kitchenette for pickup, Nichole reminded them they had one more stop to make. "Don't forget Mrs. Bandler," she said. "I can't wait to find out whether she and that handsome French doctor ever saw each other again!"

"Or whether that young soldier with the missing brother

ever found him," Shelley added, hurrying to the elevator. When it had carried them to the third floor, the JVs piled off and nearly walked right into Mrs. Bandler.

"Mrs. B!" said Bernie, surprised. "What are you doing out of bed?"

"Practicing," Mrs. Bandler told them, smiling.

"For what?" they all wanted to know.

"For my talk with your History Club," the old woman explained, her eyes bright and alert. "The doctor said I could meet with them in the visitors' lounge and I intend to walk there, not be pushed in a wheelchair." She winked at her young visitors. "It makes a better impression, don't you think?"

Delighted to see their friend out of her room, the girls walked with her to the lounge and all four spread out on chairs and a sofa. "Now," said Mrs. Bandler, pulling the belt on her ruffled robe tight, "instead of my doing all the talking, I want to hear what you girls have been up to. Tell me everything."

And they did. Mrs. Bandler was so easy to talk to that Shelley was soon swapping recipes and Nichole was confessing her latest crush. Finally, when it was Bernie's turn, she knew just what she wanted to talk about. "You were a nurse, Mrs. B," she said. "I need your professional advice."

She told Mrs. Bandler all about Roger: how he couldn't make beds, couldn't walk down the hall without attracting trouble, and about how much he needed to feel good about himself.

"That's easy," their elderly friend told her. "In the war, we learned right away that not everyone needs to be on the front line."

"What do you mean?" asked Shelley.

"I mean your friend can be lots of help doing things that don't require coordination. In fact, there are plenty of workers in a hospital who never even see a patient. But

58

their jobs are crucial—dieticians, cleaning staff, reception-
ists. There are hundreds of people the hospital couldn't
manage without.''

"And volunteers can do those jobs?" Bernie asked.

"Some of them," Mrs. Bandler told her. "We used to
call them non-contact positions.''

Bernie laughed. She thought of the way Roger attracted
accidents like a magnet. "That's just what he needs," she
said. She was so glad she'd taken her problem to Mrs. B.
She certainly had a way of making things right. "Thanks
for everything," she said, as a bell rang. "I guess we
should go.''

"No, you shouldn't," Mrs. Bandler said sternly as the
girls got up to leave. "You should stay right where you
are.''

"Code Nine," a voice on the hospital paging system
announced. "Code Nine, Ortho. Code Nine, Ortho.''

Shelley and Nichole and Bernie looked at each other.
Code 9! They'd heard about Code 9 in training. But suddenly everything they'd learned went right out of their
heads. "What does that mean?" asked Nichole. "What's
happening?''

"It's a patient alert," Mrs. Bandler told them calmly.
She remained seated. "It's an emergency in Orthopedics.
You mustn't use the elevators or stairs for the next five
minutes. "Why don't you sit down?''

"But we're volunteers," Bernie said, flustered. She
began to walk to the reception desk. "Shouldn't we do
something? Can't we help?''

"We were just on Ortho," Nichole said. "They probably need us now." She rushed for the elevator. But as she
did, a group of doctors raced down the hall. In front of
them, an orderly hurried along, pushing a huge, metal cabi-
net on wheels. It was filled with drawers from top to bottom and made a terrible clatter as the group rushed by.

59

"Hey!" one of the doctors barked at Nichole. "Don't you know Code Nine when you hear it?" Nichole pinned herself against the wall as the orderly rolled the big cart past her. In seconds, it had been loaded on the elevator and the door swept shut.

"*What* was that?" asked Nichole, ungluing herself from the wall.

"That was the Code Nine team," Mrs. Bandler told her. "They're taking the crash cart to the patient's room."

"Wow!" Shelley stared at the elevator door.

"Crash cart?" asked Bernie.

"Yes," Mrs. Bandler said. "It carries equipment for every emergency procedure—everything from opening a vein to starting a heart that's stopped." She looked at the three girls. "I told you that everyone can't be on the front line. The Code Nine team has been specially trained. The rest of us need to stay out of their way."

"But a patient's in trouble," Shelley insisted.

"I want to go help," Nichole decided, heading toward the stairs. "I'm going down to Ortho!"

"Wait, Nick," Bernie called after her. When Nichole turned around, she added, "Maybe Mrs. B is right. Maybe we just better stand back and let people do their jobs."

"No," Nichole told her. "I'm a JV. I'm not going to stand around and watch when I can help." She turned and disappeared down the stairs.

"Nichole! Wait!" Shelley and Bernie ran after her.

"Slow down, you two," Mrs. Bandler cautioned. "You'll only make things worse."

But the two girls weren't listening. They opened the big metal door to the stairs and clattered down behind Nichole, leaving the elderly woman behind. Mrs. Bandler watched them go. Then, shaking her head, she walked slowly back to her room.

60

6

Parlez-vous Français?

"Can we help?" Nichole asked the floor nurse. Breathless, she stood at the Ortho reception desk, flushed with excitement. "We heard the Code Nine announced upstairs."

The nurse looked at the three JVs. "How did you get down here?" she asked sharply. "Don't you know you're supposed to leave the stairs and elevators clear?"

"Well, yes," Shelley told her. "But we thought . . ."

"Next time," the nurse said, checking the monitors behind the desk, "just stay where you are. There's nothing you can do here." She got up, then hurried down the hall and disappeared into a room a few doors down the hall.

"Nick!" Shelley called, as Nichole followed after the nurse. "Don't you dare!"

But nothing was going to stop Nichole from being part of this big adventure. She walked right up to the room and stared in.

Inside, she saw the doctors, an orderly, and two nurses

61

standing around the bed by the door. "Ambu bag," a doctor called, as a nurse took some tubes and a blue bag out of the crash cart. "When did she stop breathing?" the doctor asked, as he placed a mask over the face of the young woman in the bed.

When Bernie and Shelley tiptoed up beside Nichole, they gasped. The woman was so pale that her skin nearly matched the sheets. She lay perfectly still, her blonde hair spread out across her pillow. Blood streamed from her left wrist. "She did fine in Post-Op, Doctor," one of the nurses said now. "But when we brought her back here and she shook off the anesthetic, she just went crazy."

The young doctor leaned over the bed. He was a short man with curly hair; his face was unshaven and streaming with perspiration as he administered the oxygen. "What's with the IV?" he asked.

The nurse looked at the woman's slender arm and the bloody spot where the intravenous tube had been pulled out of her wrist. "I told you, Doctor," she said. "The patient went crazy. She started yelling and screaming; then she tore the IV right out of her arm!"

"She's lost a lot of fluid," the doctor announced. "Let's get that back in." Quickly, the team went to work. Soon the IV was back in place and, as everyone watched tensely, the woman's eyes began to flutter and she started to cough.

"She's breathing!" the floor nurse cried. The whole room cheered and someone applauded. But as soon as the patient was fully awake and saw the people around her, she tore off the oxygen mask and began screaming. Desperately agitated, she rolled her eyes, trying to tell them something. But no one could understand her.

The doctor looked up at the floor nurse, who stood just inside the door. "She's not speaking English," he said. "Have you got the language list?"

The nurse nodded, then headed back to the reception

desk. When she returned she was carrying a thin blue notebook. She brushed angrily past the three JVs clustered timidly outside the door. "I thought I told you girls to stay out of the way!" she barked.

Once inside the room, the nurse began flipping through the pages of the notebook. "What language, Doctor?" she asked.

The young woman was becoming more and more upset. "Mafeee," she seemed to be saying. "Ooooay mafee!" The doctor leaned toward her. "What?" he asked her. "What was that?"

"Mafeee," the woman repeated, tears in her eyes. She tossed violently in her bed. "Mafeee."

"I'm not sure what language she's speaking," the doctor said. "It sounds to me like . . ."

"French," Nichole told him. "The woman is speaking French." She folded her arms and looked smugly at the floor nurse, as all eyes turned to her. "I spent last summer in Paris," she said. "We have a vacation home there."

The nurse ignored Nichole and scanned the list in her book. "Miss Fornier in Public Relations and Dr. Daniels in the Funding Office both speak French," she announced. Then she looked worried. "Miss Fornier's on leave, though." She reached for the phone. "I'll have Dr. Daniels paged."

"You don't need to," Nichole said, forcing her way into the room and running to the side of the bed. She leaned down and took the woman's hand, then looked at the others, a worried expression on her pretty face. "In French, 'ma fille' means 'my daughter.' She's asking 'Où est ma fille?' She wants to know where her daughter is!"

The floor nurse began to understand. "That's why she got so upset as soon as she came out of the anesthetic!" She, too, went to the woman's side and began to stroke her hair, trying to soothe her. "We didn't know there was anyone else in the car. She's the only one they found."

"Car?" asked Bernie from the door. "Was she in an accident?"

"A bad one," the nurse told her. "Her car was hit broadside by a truck right near the bus station on Terry Street." She glanced at her agitated patient. "She broke a lot of bones, but she did well in surgery."

"She's not doing well now." The doctor sounded worried. He turned to Nichole. "Can you tell her we'll do our best to find her daughter?"

Suddenly, Nichole looked a lot less confident than she had a minute before. "Gee," she said. "I'm better at understanding French than I am at speaking it." She bent toward the woman and spoke slowly to her. The woman, speaking twice as fast, answered her. Then she grabbed Nichole's hand, her eyes gleaming with hope. A drop of blood fell from her bruised wrist onto the white sleeve of Nichole's blouse.

"You'd better get a pencil and paper," Nichole told the nurse. "She says her six-year-old was in the car with her." She leaned over the bed again, speaking slowly, as an orderly grabbed a pad and a pen from the desk. The woman gave long, excited answers to each question Nichole asked. "She says her daughter has blonde hair," Nichole told them. "She says it's just my color, only longer." Nichole listened intently. "And she was wearing a blue sweater with green pants." She strained forward, then stood up, looking puzzled. "I think she said the pants are corduroy, but I'm not sure."

"You're doing fine," the doctor told her. "What else?"

The woman grabbed Nichole's hand again. "She says her name is Minette," Nichole translated. "She says she loves her very much." Nichole looked up, a stricken expression on her face. "She says if we don't find her, she'll die!"

"Tell her it's okay." Bernie rushed to Nichole's side. "Tell her we'll find her little girl." She grabbed Shelley's hand and raced toward the exit. "If it takes all night, we'll find Minette!"

"Wait for me!" Nichole let go of the woman's hand gently. "Trouverons votre fille," she promised. "We'll find your daughter." Then she joined her friends as they headed out the door.

"Hey!" the doctor called after them. "Let the police do that."

"Don't waste your breath," the floor nurse told him, watching the JVs race off down the street. "Those three don't follow directions."

"Gosh!" said Nichole when they'd reached the corner. "This is just like TV."

"No, it's not," Bernie reminded her. "It's real." She thought of her own little sisters and brother, safe at home. "And that means there's a real little girl out there somewhere, scared to death."

Shelley led the way across the street, then stopped. "The bus station is too far to walk," she announced. "We'd better get a ride."

"Good idea, Shell," Bernie agreed. "We'll ask my folks." They turned back and headed up the street again. In minutes the three friends were rushing breathlessly into the O'Connor living room. There, in the middle of the floor, with Mathew riding him like a horse, they found Roger.

"Hi," the handsome freshman said, looking up at Bernie from all fours. "Glad you're back."

"What on earth are you doing here?" Bernie asked.

"Play cowboys," said two-and-a-half-year-old Mathew.

65

He kicked Roger's ribs with his pajama feet. "Go, Horsie!" he yelled. "Go, Horsie!"

"Go easy, cowpoke." Roger laughed and collapsed to the floor, then grabbed Mathew, swinging him easily off his feet. Finally, he stood next to Bernie, the squirming redhead in his arms. "I needed to talk," he said shyly. "Your mom said you'd be home any minute."

"And I'll bet you didn't know how long a minute could be, did you?" Mary O'Connor, with Tracy, Sara, and Kelly in tow, walked into the room. "Thanks for keeping an eye on Matt while I got the rest of the crew ready for bed, Roger."

Bernie wondered what Roger wanted to discuss. Had he changed his mind about Mercy? Whatever it was, it would have to wait. Right now, there was a lost little girl to find! "Mom, we need your help," she announced. "And we need it fast!" As Roger and her mother and younger sisters gathered around, Bernie told them about the Code 9 alarm. And Nichole described Minette's mother and how upset she'd been.

"We've just got to find her, Mrs. O'Connor!" Shelley said. "It's getting dark, and Minette can't even speak English!"

"That's right," Nichole added. "She must have wandered away from the crash before help arrived." Suddenly, she thought of something awful. "Why, she might be hurt herself, in shock or bleeding!"

"Where did you say the accident happened?" Mrs. O'Connor, pulling a coat from the closet, was already headed for the door.

"The bus station, Mom," Bernie told her. "On Terry."

"Okay," her mother said. "Now, who's going to volunteer to babysit the younger set while the rest of us form a search party?"

"I guess I will, Mrs. O'Connor," Roger said. "After all," he added, smiling, "I'm already broken in."

"No!" Mathew surprised everyone by wriggling out of Roger's hold and running to Shelley's side. "Shelley stay," he begged her, tugging at her arm. "Shelley stay!"

"I think I'm elected," said Shelley good-naturedly.

Nichole grinned. "I don't know what it is about Shelley and younger men," she said. "They all have a crush on her."

"Maybe it's because I wish I had some brothers or sisters," Shelley said, scooping up a storybook from the floor and settling with Mathew on her lap. "It gets pretty lonely with just Clarisse and me." Clarisse, Shelley's gray tabby cat, kept her company at night while her dad worked the late shift.

The younger girls kissed their mother goodnight, and soon the search party was on the road. Roger sat up front with Mrs. O'Connor, while Bernie and Nichole shouted directions from the backseat. "Slow down, Mom!" Bernie said as they passed a group of children in a park by the bus station. "Maybe she's found some friends." Eagerly, they scanned the faces in the group, but there were only two girls and they were much too old to be Minette. "Wait!" called Nichole "Stop here!" As the car pulled to a halt by the dry cleaners, the impulsive girl leaped to the curb.

"Look!" Nichole pointed as a small girl with long blonde hair and green pants disappeared into the alleyway between stores. Now she ran down the narrow, dark street. "Better go with her," Mrs. O'Connor advised. Bernie and Roger tumbled out of the car and ran after their friend.

"Excuse me!" Nichole called after the little figure she spotted going into a door at the end of the alley. "Can I talk to you?"

The child turned now, and the three teens could see that

she wore a blue sweater! Her full curls and her big eyes made her look just like a smaller version of Nichole. But when she opened her mouth, they knew they had the wrong little girl. "What do you want?" the child asked in perfect English. She stared in fascination at Nichole's and Bernie's striped uniforms. "Mommy!" she yelled into the door. "There's nurses out here."

Disappointed, the trio started to leave. But Bernie held them back. "Wait," she said. "Let's give Minette's description to the mother. The more people looking for her the better."

The little girl's mother promised she'd be on the lookout for Minette, and the search party piled back into the car. For the next several hours, they drove up and down the roads around the bus station, with no luck. The later it got, the fewer children they saw on the street. "Where could she be?" asked Nichole. "She's only five. She can't have walked too far."

"Maybe someone gave her a ride," suggested Roger.

"If so," Mrs. O'Connor told them, "they would have reported her found by now."

"That's right!" said Bernie. "Maybe we're driving around for nothing."

"Let's call the police and find out." Mrs. O'Connor drove to a pay phone and made a call. When she came back to the car, she wore a worried look. "No," she said, "they haven't found her yet." She paused. "I hope she didn't find the wrong kind of ride."

Bernie hated to think of what might happen to a little, lost child who couldn't ask for help. She was glad her younger sisters knew never to talk to strangers. She thought of Sara and Kelly and Tracy snug at home. And then she got her brainstorm. "Wait a minute," she told the others. "I think we need to call in some experts on this case."

"What do you mean?" asked her mother.

Bernie hoped her plan would work. "Let's start back home," she said. "I'll tell you on the way."

It was nearly nine when the discouraged search party pulled into the O'Connor driveway. Through the window, they could see Shelley and Frank O'Connor in the living room. "Everyone in bed?" asked Bernie's mother, as the teens sank exhausted onto the couch.

"Sound asleep," Shelley reported, putting some stray toys into a cubby by the TV. "I've just been filling Mr. O'Connor in on what happened." She looked at their tired faces. "No luck?"

"I'm afraid not," Mrs. O'Connor told her. "But Bernie thinks we need some inside advice." She smiled, then turned to her eldest daughter. "Okay, Honey. Go wake up the experts!"

Mr. O'Connor looked surprised. "What?" he asked. "It took us two stories and six glasses of juice to get them in bed!"

"I can believe it," Roger told him. "That Mathew sure likes grape punch!"

When Bernie came downstairs with her two youngest sisters, the little girls looked around the living room, rubbing their eyes and blinking in the bright light. "We want to help, Mommy!" Sara said, running to her mother. "Do I really get to ride in the car in my nightie?" asked Kelly, her eyes shining.

"I hope this works," Bernie's mother said, getting two more coats out of the closet. "Now, button up tight, girls."

"What works?" asked Mr. O'Connor. "What's going on?"

"It's just that Minette is right around Sara and Kelly's age, Dad," Bernie explained. "She's six."

"I'm older," Sara announced proudly.

69

"I'm five," Kelly said, fumbling with the big buttons on her coat.

"And, well, I don't think anyone could crawl inside Minette's mind better than these two," Bernie said.

"It's worth a try," Nichole told him. "We tried everything else we could think of."

"And we came up empty," Mrs. O'Connor concluded. "Maybe these two will think of something we didn't."

Mr. O'Connor stood and opened the door. "Okay," he told his wife. "But I'll take the second driving shift. You look bushed."

"I am," Bernie's mother confessed.

"Good. You join Matt and Tracy in dreamland," he said. "And we'll be back with the little mademoiselle." He kissed her, picked Kelly up in his arms, and led the way outside. "Come on, Shelley," he called over his shoulder. "You're on the second shift with me."

"You're not leaving us behind," Nichole said, rushing out the door with the other teens behind her. "Wait for me!" shouted Sara. "I still have my bedroom slippers on, and I can't ..." Before she could finish, Roger had scooped her up and carried her, giggling happily, to the car.

They hadn't driven halfway to the bus station when Sara and Kelly saw the huge neon elephant. He was rearing up on his back legs and his trunk was showering electronic sprays of blue and pink water. Underneath him, yellow letters announced, JUMBO'S BURGERS. GRAND OPENING. "Daddy! Daddy!" shouted Kelly. "Look at the elephant." Beside her, Sara turned to press her face against the car window. "I want to stop here, Daddy. Can we stop here?"

"We haven't got time to eat, girls," Mr. O'Connor told them, slowing the car to look at the sign. "We have a little girl to find."

70

"Please!" Sara begged. "Please!"

Bernie looked at the colorful sign, turning slowly on its axis, and the circus posters that decorated the windows of Jumbo's. Just outside the door stood the statue of a clown, his hand raised to wave, his floppy hat topped with a yellow flower. "Maybe we should stop, Dad," she said. "I mean this is certainly the kind of place I'd come to if I were six." She turned to her friends, who were all studying Ridge Dale's newest fast food spot.

"It's too far from the bus station," Roger decided. "Why would a little kid come all the way out here?"

"I want to see the elephant up close," begged Kelly, trying to open the car door. "I want to see the elephant."

"What if that's just what Minette wanted?" asked Bernie, watching the bright elephant revolve slowly in the dark sky.

"She's right!" Shelley opened the car and stood outside, looking up at the sign. "I bet you can see this elephant for miles." She helped Kelly out and held her up to see. "It shines like a star!" the little girl said, raising her hands toward the bright lights.

"Let's take a look, then." Mr. O'Connor got out, too, and opened the door for the rest. "It's a chance, even if it's a small one." He walked briskly into the restaurant, the teens right behind him. All of them filed past the clown, although Kelly stopped to touch his gloved hand. "Hello," she said politely as she followed the others in.

The inside of Jumbo's was as colorful as the outside. The plastic booths were bright red and the tables were painted green. Above every table was a light in the shape of a circus tent. And, of course, in the center of the restaurant, right beside the counter, was a replica of an elephant. He stood on his back legs, his trunk raised just like the elephant on the sign. Beside him, chewing on a long lock

71

of golden hair, stood a small girl who looked at them with frightened eyes. She wore a blue sweater and green pants.

Nichole knelt beside her, trying not to startle her. She put her arms around the little waist. ''Bon soir,'' she said. ''Minette?'' The others held their breath as the child looked solemnly at Nichole. ''Où est Maman?'' she asked in a quavering voice.

Nichole grinned at her friends with relief. ''She speaks French,'' she said, happily.

Shelley and Bernie hugged each other. ''What did she say?'' Roger asked.

Nichole stood up. ''She asked, 'Where is my Momma?' '' she told them. Then the little runaway took her by the hand and pulled her down to whisper something else in her ear.

''What is it?'' asked Bernie. ''What does she want?''

Nichole picked the child up and carried her to the counter. ''Two hamburgers,'' she told them, ''and a choco-late shake.''

7

The Best Medicine

"It's awfully late," Shelley whispered, as the mechanical doors swept open in front of them. "Visiting hours have been over forever."

"I'll bet they'll make an exception in this case," Mr. O'Connor told her. In his arms he carried Minette, full of hamburgers and sound asleep. "The police and the social service people phoned the hospital. Mrs. Charpentier isn't doing so well, and everyone agreed that seeing her daughter is probably the best medicine she could get."

Bernie and her friends followed her father down the deserted corridors of Mercy. They had stopped at the O'Connors' to drop the little ones off and to phone the police. Now, as they approached the main elevator, Bernie was worried. "You didn't tell us Minette's mom was worse, Dad," she said. "What's wrong?"

They all filed into the empty elevator car, and Roger pushed the button for the second floor. "They don't seem to know," Mr. O'Connor told them. "She's got a lot of broken bones, but that doesn't explain why she keeps slipping in and out of consciousness.'' He looked at the sleeping child, then at the teens. ''They're worried about brain damage.''

''Oh, no!'' Nichole remembered the little girl's first question. ''Where is my mama?'' she had asked. ''Suppose she doesn't wake up?''

Shelley led the way to the reception desk for the Ortho Unit. ''Hi,'' she told the nurse there. ''We have Mrs. Charpentier's daughter with us. Can we see her?''

The nurse glanced at Minette and smiled. ''Of course,'' she said. ''But I'm afraid she won't know her. She's not responding to anything.''

''Will she be all right?''

The nurse shook her head. ''I don't know,'' she said. ''I just don't know.''

Gently, Nichole leaned over Minette. ''Ta mere est ici, Minette,'' she said. ''Your mother is here.''

The little girl's eyes snapped open. ''Maman?'' she asked. Mr. O'Connor put her down and she took Nichole's hand, tugging her ahead. The nurse smiled, then walked ahead of them toward Mrs. Charpentier's room. Eagerly, the others followed Nichole and Minette down the hall.

''I'm sorry,'' the nurse turned back to them. ''Only one person can go in with her. Mrs. Charpentier is in serious condition.''

Mr. O'Connor nodded to Nichole. ''You go ahead,'' he told her. ''We can't speak French.'' Reluctantly, the other teens found seats in the small waiting room behind the desk. ''I'm too worked up to sit,'' Bernie's father told them. He watched the nurse lead Nichole and Minette into a room down the hall, then began walking back and forth across the room.

Roger looked around him. He saw the worried expressions on his friends' faces, felt the tension in the small room. He remembered when he'd been admitted to Mercy with his broken arm. "Boy," he told Bernie and Shelley, "I think I'd rather be a patient than wait like this!"

"I just hope everything works out," Bernie said. She felt tears start up in her eyes. "That poor little girl."

The clock on the wall seemed to crawl as the four of them waited. Occasionally, an announcement over the hospital intercom broke the silence. Everyone looked up when another nurse came to take over the reception desk. But she had no news, and they began to tire. It was after midnight, and the teens would have to get up early for school. Bernie folded her coat into a pillow and put her head down on one arm of her chair. Roger propped his feet up on a second chair, and drifted off to sleep.

It seemed like hours later when Shelley's excited shout woke them. "Nichole!" Bernie opened her eyes and everyone turned to see Nichole and the floor nurse coming toward them down the hall. They jumped from their seats and gathered around her. "What happened?" "How is she?" "Where's Minette?"

Nichole sank into a chair. Her uniform, after the long day, had lost its fresh, crisp look. Her hair, piled on top of her head in a neat knot while she worked at Mercy, was now loose from its clip and falling in lank strands around her tear-streaked face. "It's terrible," she told them. "Minette keeps talking to her, but she won't wake up."

"Oh, Nick!" Bernie couldn't believe it. "Is Minette upset?"

Nichole wiped her eyes. "Not as much as I am, I guess," she told Bernie. "She won't give up. She sits there holding her mother's hand." Nichole stopped, and for a minute it looked as if she were about to cry again. "She says her mama's taking a nap."

"One of you may go in now, if you want," said the

75

nurse, kindly. "I've set up a cot in the room for the little girl."

Bernie put her hand on Nichole's shoulder. "I'll go," she said.

Mr. O'Connor looked at his watch. "You all have school in the morning," he reminded them. "I think we should come back tomorrow."

"I'll just peek in," Bernie promised, looking pleadingly at her father. "I'll be right back." Mr. O'Connor nodded, the others settled back in their chairs, and Bernie started down the hall.

When she walked into Mrs. Charpentier's room, everything was dark and still. In the light from the hall, Bernie could see the small cot set up by the bed, the IV pole, and the machine they'd wheeled in to keep track of Mrs. Charpentier's vital signs. It looked as though both the patient and her daughter were sound asleep. But just as she was about to leave, the little figure in the cot sat up, rubbing her eyes. "Allo," Minette told her.

"Hello," Bernie replied, walking back into the room and sitting down on the foot of Minette's cot. Little Minette looked like a doll, a very sleepy doll. Her cheeks were flushed and her long blonde hair tumbled over her shoulders. Bernie couldn't speak French, but she was used to putting sleepy little girls to bed. "I think it's time you were asleep, young lady," she said.

Minette pointed to her mother, who lay motionless in the bed. "Shhhhh," she said, laying a finger across her lips. Then with her other hand, she softly stroked her mother's wrist. In a tiny voice, she began to sing.

Bernie couldn't understand the words, but she recognized the lullaby that Minette was crooning to her mother. It was "Rockabye Baby!" Gently, she picked the child up and held her in her lap by her mother's side, and began to sing with her. "Rockabye baby, on the tree top," she

76

sang in a whisper. "When the wind blows the cradle will rock . . ."

As if she heard the music, Mrs. Charpentier moved her hand. Swaying to the rhythm, the fingers of her hand trembled. Bernie thought maybe she was imagining it. She kept singing, wondering if Minette noticed. "When the bough breaks," they sang, "the cradle will fall . . ."

It was no mistake! Mrs. Charpentier opened her eyes and looked at them. "Down will come baby, cradle and all." Minette reached across her mother's IV tube and hugged the pretty woman. As if she had just woken from a brief nap, Mrs. Charpentier laughed. "Minette," she said, her voice full of love.

"Quick! Quick!" Bernie raced out into the hall. "Come quick!" In her excitement, she forgot to use the call button. She forgot not to yell in the hospital corridor. She forgot everything but the wonderful, amazing miracle that had just taken place.

"She's awake!" she told the nurse, who rushed down the hall. Mr. O'Connor and Bernie's friends hurried after her. "We were singing "Rockabye Baby" and she heard us." Bernie hugged her father. "She was moving her hands to the music." She hugged Shelley and Nichole and Roger. "And she woke up. She woke up!"

The scene that followed was a happy, confusing one. Mrs. Charpentier was very excited and speaking too fast for Nichole to understand. The only word she clearly heard, over and over, was "Merci" or "Thank you." Minette, thrilled to have her mother back, was standing on the bed, hugging first Mrs. Charpentier, then her new teen friends. For Mr. O'Connor, she had a big kiss. The nurse begged the little girl to calm down so she could examine her patient, and Bernie turned to everyone, dizzy with delight. "You see?" she asked. "I told you! I told you!"

In the car, the friends were much too happy to sleep.

As Mr. O'Connor headed for home, they couldn't stop reviewing the thrilling events of the day. "I can hardly believe it!" said Nichole. "Everything worked out like a storybook!"

"It sure did," agreed Shelley. "We just watched the absolute happiest ending of all time!"

"The only trouble with this story," Roger said, stretching his long legs and yawning, "is that the next chapter takes place at eight A.M. in school!"

Mr. O'Connor didn't like the thought of getting up for work, either. "It's been a long night," he agreed. "And I think you four deserve to take the day off tomorrow if you want."

"I can't," Bernie said. "I've got a math test."

"Me, too," said Roger. "And Mrs. Vickers' tests are really rough."

"I'm in the same class," chimed in Shelley. "But you're not," she added, turning to Nichole. "Why don't you take the day off?"

"I can't either," wailed Nichole. "Believe it or not, I've got a French test!"

Everyone in the car burst out laughing. "Don't worry, Nick," Roger told her. "You should do great. You just got plenty of practice!"

As they neared their first stop, the fabulous Peters' mansion, Bernie suddenly remembered. "Hey, Roger," she asked her sleepy friend in the front seat, "what was it you came over to see me about tonight?"

Roger put his arm on the back of the seat and turned to face the three girls behind him. "It was about Mercy," he said.

"Did you change your mind about volunteering?" Nichole asked.

"Not really," confessed Roger. "I just came over to tell Bernie I was sorry for being such a jerk."

Bernie sighed. She wished she hadn't pushed Roger into the training. He certainly didn't need other people to decide what was right for him!

Now Roger smiled broadly. "But that was before tonight," he told them.

"What?" Bernie stared at her friend. "What do you mean, Rog?"

"Tonight was pretty special," Roger told her. "And the special part wasn't just the excitement. It was, well . . . the . . ."

"Happy ending?" Nichole finished for him.

Roger grinned. Suddenly he didn't look tired at all. "That's right," he agreed. "I mean, I may not be cut out to push wheelchairs." He remembered the look of joy on Minette's face when her mother held her in her arms. "But there must be something I can do. Some way I can help make things like tonight happen."

"There is!" Bernie looked at Shelley and Nichole. "Remember what Mrs. B told us about non-contact positions?"

The girls thought back over their busy day. It seemed like ages ago that they'd had their visit with Harriet Bandler. "Of course!" remembered Shelley. "You don't need to be on the front lines to fight a war, Roger."

"Huh?" Roger looked confused.

"She means there are plenty of jobs in a big hospital like Mercy," Bernie said. "And lots of them don't involve patient contact at all."

"Sure," Nichole told him. "Did you know they use volunteers to catalog books in the medical library? Heck, it's usually a volunteer who answers the phone when you call. They type, file, run messages—just about everything."

"Hey," said Roger, "I don't care if I wash dishes or scrub floors. Just so I can help."

"Rog, that's great," Nichole told him, as Mr. O'Connor

79

drove the car up the Peters' long, curving driveway and stopped in front of the stately home. "But maybe you ought to skip the dishes part?"

Again, the car's passengers burst into laughter, as everyone imagined the damage Roger could do if he got his hands on hundreds of plates and glasses. "Okay," the good-humored boy agreed. "But you'll see. I'm going to finish the training this weekend. And then I'm going to give Mercy one hundred percent!"

Bernie was proud of her friend. She saw the look of determination on his handsome face, and she knew it was true. Somehow, some way, Roger was going to become part of their JV team.

"Some Friday night!" Teddy complained. "All my friends are so tired they can hardly stand up!"

It was true. The gang had gone to Pizza Paradise after school, but the four members of Minette's "rescue team" could hardly keep their eyes open. "Sorry, Teddy," Roger said. "But we didn't get much sleep last night."

"You try looking for a lost child until all hours and then studying for a hideous French test," Nichole said.

"Or a hideous math test," Shelley added.

"Well, it sounds like you did a great job," Teddy told them. "If I didn't have to work in my dad's auto body shop, I'd have been with you." He twisted his mouth in a tragic grimace. "I missed the film opportunity of a lifetime."

"Is that all you ever think about?" Nichole asked.

"No," Teddy insisted. "I think about other important things, too." He counted on his hand. "There's gorgeous females." He grinned at Nichole. "Then there's pizza, double-thick chocolate shakes, and gorgeous females."

Nichole rolled her blue eyes and folded her arms. "Well, I'm thinking about how wonderful it is that Minette and her mother are together again. Those two really have something to be grateful for this Thanksgiving.''

''I wish I did,'' groaned Shelley. ''Everyone else is happy about getting out of school and having a big, fat turkey dinner.'' She sighed. ''But all I can think about is that I've got all those pies and tarts to make before next Thursday!''

''You'll do fine,'' Bernie told her. ''Everything you make always tastes super delicious.'' She looked up as their waiter laid a tray of Deluxe pizza on their table. ''In fact,'' she offered, ''if I get to eat the leftovers, I hereby volunteer to help you cook.'' She reached for a slice of the cheese-covered pie.

''Me, too,'' Nichole said. ''I adore pumpkin! Next to strawberry, it's my favorite flavor!''

''Add another volunteer to your list,'' Teddy told Shelley. ''If there's food involved, count me in.''

''That goes double for me,'' smiled Roger. ''My mom's still on a diet, and we don't get seconds or desserts at my house!''

Shelley laughed. ''You're all great,'' she said. ''I can't believe how much the extra money from my catering business has meant to Dad and me.'' She looked at her friends. ''Dad says he might even be able to switch to the day shift.''

''Oh, Shell,'' said Bernie, ''that's wonderful!'' She knew how lonely Shelley got with only her cat for company at night. She couldn't imagine what it would be like to eat dinner alone without her noisy, funny family gathered around the table.

''Okay,'' announced Shelley happily. ''It's a date. Let's meet at my house on Monday after school. That way I can deliver everything to the Mercy snack bar on Wednesday.'' She sipped her soda, then grinned at the gang. ''I'm serving refreshments for the cooks!''

"Deal," said Teddy enthusiastically. "Sounds like a job I could really sink my teeth into!"

"I work at Mercy after school on Monday," Nichole said. "But I'll come over as soon as I'm finished." She brightened with a sudden thought. "Maybe I could bring Julie and some of the others if they're on duty, too."

"Too many cooks *can't* spoil my soup," said Shelley. "Especially since I'm making pies!" She smiled gratefully at Nichole. "That would be terrific, Nick. Thanks."

The teens talked about the busy week ahead. They had two hundred pies and tarts to bake on Monday, and Mrs. Bandler was supposed to talk to the History Club on Wednesday! "I asked Bev if we could come even though we're not members," Bernie told them. "She said Mr. Haggerty is chartering a bus to go to the hospital and all we have to do is sign up."

"Great," Roger said. "After everything you three have told me about Mrs. Bandler, I can't wait to meet her."

"Not me," said Teddy. "Old people make me uncomfortable. Especially old ladies." He shuddered. "My great-aunt Elizabeth wears too much makeup and she hugs me so hard I'm surprised her false teeth don't fall out." He paused. "In fact, I'm surprised *my* teeth don't fall out."

Everyone laughed. "Mrs. B isn't like that at all," Shelley told him. "She's just about the smartest, hippest old person I've ever met."

"And the war stories she tells would make great movies," Nichole added.

"They would?" Suddenly, Teddy looked interested. "Do you think she'd work with an unknown filmmaker?"

Nichole giggled. "Why don't you come to the meeting and see?" she asked.

"Wow!" Teddy was off on a fantasy trip, writing film titles in the air. "*Guns and Guts,* written by Theodore

Hollins, produced by Theodore Hollins, directed by Theodore Hollins."

"And what about Mrs. B?" asked Nichole.

"Story Consultant, Harriet Bandler," Teddy added quickly. Then, he looked at his watch and leaped to his feet. "Enough talk. Now it's time to get some directing tips from one of the hottest film talents around." He grinned at the gang. "Come on, guys," he urged. "It's time for the early show at the Cineplex. I've been waiting for *Revenge of the Mutant Porcupines* all week! It's directed by Peter Sheldon, the modern master of special effects." He rose from his seat and headed for the door. But no one got up to follow him. "Come on," he repeated. "We don't want to be late. There are four murders in the first three minutes."

Roger yawned. "Sorry, Ted," he said. "This puppy's headed for bed. I am bushed!"

"Me, too," Nichole said, covering her hand with her mouth. "Unless that movie stars Corey Hudson, I'm not interested." She struggled into her plush pink coat. "The only thing I want right now is about seventy hours of sleep!"

"But we made plans," Teddy objected. "It's Friday night." He looked at his exhausted friends. "Time to party!"

"Sorry, Teddy," Bernie told him. "But partying is out for tonight. None of us got any sleep last night."

"Shelley?" Teddy looked at his last hope. "Shelley?"

But Shelley didn't answer. Her head on her hands, she sat slumped against the wall. She had fallen asleep!

8

Fire!

"It's for you, Bernie." Mr. O'Connor, who had picked up the phone in the living room, peered into the kitchen where Bernie and her mother were finishing the Sunday dinner dishes. "Of course," he added, "it always is." He often teased his eldest daughter that if they gave credit in school for phone conversations, she would be number one in her class!

Bernie ran into the living room and took the phone from her father. It was Roger. "Training was great!" he told her. "I'm going to make up the day I missed on Thursday, and then Mrs. Hurley says I'll be an official JV."

"Oh, Rog," Bernie told him. "That's terrific." She turned to her father, handing him the phone. "I'll take it upstairs," she told him.

She raced to the hall phone on the second floor, then dragged its extra-long cord into her room and closed the door. When her father had hung up she demanded, "Tell me everything!"

"Well," Roger told her, "I still can't make a bed."

Bernie laughed. "If you're smart," she said, "you'll never learn! I made thirteen today."

"But I got through the day without dropping, cracking, or exploding anything." Roger sighed contentedly. "So I figure I'm way ahead." Bernie could almost see his broad grin. "I think Mrs. Hurley does, too!"

Bernie lay down across her apple-green bedspread. She looked above her at her ceiling stars. They were already glowing dimly in the early evening light. "Maybe we'll be working together by Thursday!" She could hardly believe her dream of working side by side with Roger might come true.

"I don't think so, Bern," Roger said. "I mean, I just wouldn't trust myself around patients." For a minute he sounded solemn, but then his tone lightened. "Mrs. Hurley says she's going to start a Paper Patrol, a squad of volunteers who don't work on the units. Instead, we'll help out in the hospital offices. You know—carry messages, file, type—stuff like that."

"Gee, Rog," Bernie said, disappointed. "Are you sure that's what you want?"

"Hey," he assured her, "what I want is to help. If that means pushing papers, then I'll do it!"

She knew he was right. It was just like Mrs. B had said. Not everyone needed to be on the front lines. They talked a while longer, and when Roger hung up, she felt glad he'd found a place at Mercy at last. She lay on her back for a few minutes, without the energy to get up and put her nightgown on. She was just beginning to drift off to sleep when the phone on the bed beside her rang sharply.

At first, Bernie couldn't figure out why there was a horrible, loud ringing in her ears. Finally, groggy with sleep, she picked up the receiver. "Hello."

"Bernie?" Shelley's voice sounded urgent. Bernie snapped awake.

"What's the matter, Shell? What is it?" she asked.

"Bernie, you have to come quick! Something terrible's happened!"

Bernie could hear voices, men's voices in the background. She knew Shelley spent most nights alone with Clarisse. "Who's there?" she asked.

"The firemen," Shelley told her.

"What?" Now Bernie was *really* awake. She sat up in the middle of her bed, grabbing the phone with both hands.

"Oh, Bernie," Shelley wailed. "I've burnt the house down!"

"Wait a minute," Bernie said. "Do you mean you're at the firehouse?" She pictured Shelley at the new Ridge Dale firehouse, huddled in a blanket, a tiny bundle of precious belongings beside her.

"No, I'm home," Shelley told her. "It's really just the kitchen I totaled." Shelley sniffed. "I was trying to get a head start on the pie fillings for tomorrow. I put some milk on the stove to scald and sat down in the living room to read." Shelley's voice trembled. "I guess I fell asleep. The next thing I knew, Clarisse was licking my face and there was this awful smell everywhere."

Bernie sighed with relief. Things weren't as desperate as Shelley had made them sound. "Everything's going to be okay," she said soothingly. "We'll have things cleaned up in no time. Does your dad know?"

"They called him at work," Shelley explained. "But he couldn't come to the phone. There was some emergency at the factory." Shelley's voice trembled. "Oh, Bernie, what am I going to do? The firemen disconnected the stove. They say it's too dangerous to use!"

"Stay there. I'll be right over." Bernie hung up and went to tell her family. Mrs. O'Connor drove her over to

Shelley's, and armed with rags, mops, and three bottles of household cleaner, the two of them walked into the kitchen to inspect the damage.

The walls and floors were covered with soot, the wallpaper had buckled in several places, and there was a big black, cloud-shaped stain behind the stove. But it was the stove itself that had really borne the brunt of the fire. The porcelain finish was the color of marshmallows that have been toasted too long, and the top burners had collapsed in on themselves as if the stove had been folded in half. It looked like a dollhouse toy someone had decided to squash!

Mrs. O'Connor whistled softly. "Well," she said, "we can get the room back in shape for you, Shelley. But I think the Jansens are going to be in the market for a new stove."

Bernie saw the look on her friend's face. "Don't worry," she said, putting her arm around Shelley, "we can meet at my house tomorrow and still get everything done."

"Tomorrow?" Bernie's mother asked.

"Yep," Bernie told her. "We're all going to pitch in and help Shelley's Catering cook up a Thanksgiving feast!"

"Not at our house, I'm afraid." Mrs. O'Connor sprayed a cloth with cleaner and started in on one of the walls. "Not unless you want to fight for the stove with twenty-five Brownies. Tracy's troop is baking cookies for our fundraiser tomorrow."

Shelley took the mop Bernie handed her, but she didn't use it. Instead, she sat down on a chair beside the small, round breakfast table. "This has been positively the worst day of my life!" she said. Softly, she called to Clarisse, who wandered out of the dining room on her padded feet, then hopped onto Shelley's lap. "And it's not going to get any better when Dad comes home."

"When *who* comes home?" asked a voice behind them. Everyone turned as Mark Jansen, a slender, dark-haired man in a blue work shirt, walked into the kitchen. "Wow!" he said, looking around the room. "When you cook up trouble, Shelley Jansen, you don't go halfway!"

"Dad!" Shelley stood up from her chair, and Clarisse jumped to the floor with an indignant meow. "What are you doing home?"

Shelley's father gave her a hug. "They told me there'd been a fire," he said. "They said you weren't hurt, but I was afraid you might be pretty shaken up."

Shelley nuzzled gratefully into her father's shoulders. "Oh, Dad," she said, "I'm just so sorry I made such a mess!"

"It's not as bad as it looks, Mark," Bernie's mother told him. "Nothing a little elbow grease won't make good as new." She looked at the crumpled stove. "With one exception," she added quickly.

Shelley, too, turned to stare at the ruined stove. "I'm afraid Shelley's Catering is out of business," she said miserably.

Mr. Jansen took his daughter by both shoulders. "It most certainly is not," he said firmly. "The staff is on temporary leave until we buy another stove." He kissed her on the forehead. "We needed a new one, anyway."

"Gosh," Shelley said. "I thought you'd be mad."

"I'm just glad you're all right," Mr. Jansen told her. "It's a lot easier to replace a stove than a cook." He winked at Bernie and her mother. "Now, how about handing me one of those mops?"

"My dad was great," Shelley told the gang at lunch next day. "But you should have seen the mess!" She turned to her redheaded friend. "Right, Bern?"

88

Bernie smiled. "Let's just say the Jansen kitchen isn't going to make this month's cover of *House Beautiful*," she said.

"So where are we having our cooking party tonight?" asked Teddy. He swallowed a forkful of chicken salad. "I could sure use some real food!"

"If you need an extra hand," volunteered Bev Feldon, "count me in."

"An extra stove is what we really need," Bernie told her. "Would your mom mind if we worked at your house? Mine's going to be full of ten-year-olds."

"Well," said Bev, "I guess . . ."

"Why not use my house?" Roger looked as though he could already smell pies and cakes hot out of the stove. "If my mom is around while we're cooking, maybe she'll go off her diet and we can start eating like people instead of rabbits at our house."

"We could get a lot more done at *my* house," Nichole insisted. "We have a double oven and a three-door refrigerator." She brushed sandwich crumbs from the lap of her Mercy uniform. "Besides, our cook can stay and help."

"Gee," said Shelley. "Thanks. I guess . . ."

"No offense, Nichole," Elise Sheridan interrupted, "but your kitchen can't compare to mine."

"What?" Nichole looked in surprise at her round-faced friend. Everyone knew that Nichole's architect father and mother had imported the finest kitchen appliances and cookware from France.

"Well, maybe it's not *my* kitchen exactly," Elise admitted. "But I *do* practically live there." She grinned. "I mean my dad's bakery. It's the perfect place to bake by the hundreds." She counted off all the advantages on her chubby fingers. "It's got a giant brick oven, restaurant-size cooling racks, all the sugar and flour and eggs you

89

could ever need, *and* the best pastry cook in the world as consultant.''

''Your dad would work with us?'' Shelley was so excited she forgot all about her lunch. Everyone in town knew how scrumptious bread and cake from Sheridan's Bakery tasted. It was a Sunday morning tradition for Ridge Dale families to send one member to Sheridan's for fresh hot coffee cake or a dozen caraway bagels! ''Oh, Elise, do you think he really would?''

''It's just for one night,'' Elise told her. ''I'll phone him right after lunch.''

''Just think of all the tricks I could learn from him!'' Shelley said. ''Of course, I wouldn't ask him for any of his special secrets.''

''I'm sure he'd be glad to share anything, Shell,'' Elise assured her friend. ''Anything except the ingredients in his 'Sweet Mystery' chocolate cake, that is. I've been trying to wheedle that out of him for years, but he keeps saying I'm not ready.'' Elise laughed her bubbly, deep laugh. ''If ten years of helping him make doughnuts and cookies every day after school doesn't make me ready, I don't know what will!''

''Well, I don't care what's in that cake,'' Teddy told them. ''I just know it transports you to another dimension!''

''Yeah—Heaven!'' added Roger. ''My brother snuck one into the house last week. We pigged out up in his room. My stomach is still smiling!''

Elise stood up, taking her tray and her backpack with her. ''It's a date, then,'' she said. ''I'll go call Dad to make sure it's okay, and we'll all meet by the gym after school.''

''Thanks a bunch,'' Shelley told her.

''No problem,'' Elise said. ''It'll be fun to have other people around while I'm on doughnut duty!'' She turned and headed out of the cafeteria, leaving the others to make excited plans.

"Just think!" said Shelley dreamily. "I'll be working with a professional baker."

"And I'll be surrounded by free samples!" dreamed Teddy.

"Can we make an extra tart for Mrs. B?" asked Bernie, remembering that she and Shelley would be working at Mercy the next day.

"And how about something for Minette?" begged Nichole. "They're letting her stay right in the room with her mom. It's really helping Mrs. Charpentier recover faster." She grabbed her tray as the bell rang and the gang stood up. "The way that little kid put away hamburgers, I'll bet she could eat a whole pie by herself!"

As they dropped off their trays and headed for the door, Shelley felt very happy and very grateful. "Of course," she said. "We'll make extras for everyone. She turned to the others. "You guys are so great to help me out like this," she said quietly. "You are the best friends anybody ever had!"

Paul Sheridan was as round and full of fun as his daughter. "Well," he said when the six teens trooped into his bakery, "I see the Ridge Dale cooking varsity is ready for action."

"We sure are, Dad," Elise told him. She led her friends behind the counter and into the big kitchen at the back of the store. "Where should we start?"

"*You* start by keeping us in doughnuts, young lady," Mr. Sheridan told her. "No one makes breakfast Thanksgiving day. The whole town will be in here bright and early for doughnuts and bagels."

"But, Dad," Elise objected, "I want to help Shelley."

"The best way you can help Shelley is to free me up

91

so *I* can help her." Mr. Sheridan put his hands on his broad Santa Claus hips. "Unless, of course," he said, winking at the others, "you want to tell her how to make the flakiest pie crust on the eastern seaboard."

Soon everyone was at work on a different task. Teddy offered to help Elise make doughnuts, claiming that his artistic talents would be of special help when it came to icing them. Roger was given a sit-down job where his accident-proneness wouldn't cause too much damage. So, while Shelley and Mr. Sheridan mixed up pastry flour and shortening to make dough, and Bernie and Bev rolled it and cut it into circles for pies and tarts, Roger, his hands in transparent plastic gloves, fitted each circle carefully into a baking tin.

As they worked, the Ridge Dale cooking varsity chatted and laughed. As the big brick oven heated up, warming the huge kitchen, Shelley and Mr. Sheridan traded recipes and swapped stories of cooking triumphs and tragedies. "When school started," Shelley confided to her new ally, "I burnt a corn soufflé in my first home ec class."

"That's nothing," Mr. Sheridan told her. "I once baked a wedding cake for two hundred people with salt instead of sugar!" He laughed at the memory. "You should have seen the guests' faces!"

By the time Nichole and her friends arrived from Mercy, the filled pastry shells were heating in the oven and the team of cooks were getting ready to decorate the finished pies. Two empty Pizza Paradise boxes lay on the counter, the remains of their hurried dinner. "Mmmm!" said the blonde JV as she walked into the bakery. "It smells too good for words in here!" Following behind her, Blake Willard and Julie Hayden agreed. "If we're too late to help cook," Blake announced, "we'll be glad to lick the bowls!"

"If these pies taste half as good as they smell," Julie told him, "Mercy's snack bar will sell out!"

Mr. Sheridan bowed from the waist, then took Nichole's and Julie's coats and hung them on a hook behind the counter. "On behalf of my fellow chefs," he said, "thank you."

"You're just in time to help us decorate, guys," Shelley told her friends. While Elise's father began removing the rich caramel-colored pies from the oven, she handed Nichole a shiny metal cylinder. "Here's the pastry tube. How about some whipped cream roses on our pumpkin pies?"

Julie joined them. "Oh," she said, "can I try?" Mr. Sheridan handed her another tube, then showed the two girls how to squeeze the stiff cream into shapes. Soon Nichole was making beautiful flowers on the borders of the pies, while Julie put two little leaves on the sides of each rose. "I can't wait until Minette and Mrs. B taste these!" Nichole sighed.

"You saw them?" asked Bernie, looking up from the last batch of mincemeat filling. "How are they?"

Nichole grinned. "Not only did we see them," she told her friends, "we introduced them."

"You what?"

"Julie and I figured it was about time our two favorite Mercy patients met each other," Nichole explained.

"After all, poor little Minette is there all day," Julie added. "She has nothing to do except watch her mother do physical therapy and bug the nurses for seconds on desserts!"

Nichole moved her pastry tube around to form a lacey M on one of the tiny tarts. "And Mrs. B is getting stronger every day," she said. "We thought they'd be great company for each other.

"So I talked to Mrs. Charpentier. I asked her if I could take Minette visiting." Now she decorated another tart with a fancy whip cream B. "You should have seen those two chatter away. Mrs. B was stationed in France during the war, and her French is a lot better than mine!"

Blake watched the decorating for a while, then walked over to Roger. "Welcome to my laboratory," Roger told him, holding out his gloved hand.

"We heard you needed help," Blake said, pulling away from Roger's dough-covered handshake. "But it looks like you've got everything under control."

Roger handed Blake another pair of plastic gloves. "Dere is alvays room for vun more, Doctor," he said in his Transylvanian accent. Then he showed Blake how to fit the circles of dough into the tins, and together they finished the last few pies. "If I do say so myself," Blake said, holding up a pie, "these look terrific."

"So do these doughnuts Teddy and Elise spent all night baking!" Elise's father led his daughter and Teddy into the center of the room to show off their handiwork. They each carried a tray piled high with dozens and dozens of doughnuts of different kinds. Some were chocolate covered with white icing, others were cream-filled and iced with sprinkles. Others were covered with pink icing, and still others seemed to be striped with several colors. "I couldn't make up my mind," Teddy explained when the gang noticed his rainbow creations.

"Now that we've finished our pies, how about we celebrate with some doughnuts?" Mr. Sheridan suggested, smiling. "I don't think the owner will notice if we sneak a few!"

He didn't need to ask twice. In minutes one of the doughnut mountains had gotten a lot smaller, and eight happy teens were munching and talking. While they gossiped, Mr. Sheridan pulled Shelley to one side. "Any time you want to borrow my kitchen, Miss Jansen," he told

94

her, "you just let me know. It was a pleasure working with a fine cook like you."

Shelley looked at him gratefully. "I can't thank you enough, Mr. Sheridan," she said. "And I only hope one day I can be half as good a cook as you!"

"From the job you're doing at Mercy," he said, "I think Shelley's Catering is off to a good start." He untied the white apron from his thick waist and laid it on the counter. "But just to make sure, I'm going to give you a secret weapon." He leaned over and whispered something in her ear. Shelley's eyes widened.

After they'd cleaned up the shop and packed the trays of pies in boxes for the snack bar to pick up, the teens said good-bye to Elise and her father. Exhausted but happy, each carried a pastry box with a special treat to take home. "Boy!" said Bernie. "That was the most time I've ever spent in a kitchen. It makes me really appreciate what Mom goes through!"

"This was the best day ever!" said Shelley happily. "I feel like dancing!" She held her pastry box at arm's length and floated down the street.

"What on earth was Mr. Sheridan whispering to you about, anyway?" asked Julie. She brushed her short-clipped bangs from her eyes with one hand, careful to keep her precious box from tipping. "You looked like he told you how to win the lottery."

"He did. Sort of," Shelley said, smiling to herself.

"What do you mean, Shell?" asked Bernie.

"Well," Shelley confessed. "He gave me the recipe for 'Sweet Mystery' cake number two."

"Number two?" Teddy was surprised. "Isn't one Sweet Mystery enough for anyone?"

"Of course," Shelley explained. "But he thought I might like to make an orange version of his chocolate dream."

"Wow!" Roger picked up speed to walk between Shelley and Bernie. "If your orange cake tastes half as good as his chocolate one, you'll be famous!"

"And very popular!" Blake added. "We had a 'Sweet Mystery' cake for dinner last week, and I ate two pieces for breakfast!"

"So how do you make it?" Bernie asked, curious. "What's in this fabulous new cake of yours?"

"Sorry, guys," Shelley told them. She walked briskly ahead. "I can't tell you."

"Why on earth not?" Nichole wanted to know.

"Because," said Shelley firmly, her eyes shining with pride, "it's a professional secret!"

9

Yesterday's News

When Bernie and Shelley reported for duty at the desk on Ortho, they expected to have lots of time to visit with Mrs. Charpentier and Minette. What they hadn't counted on was all the jobs that were waiting for them. The floor nurse, a tall woman with smartly cut gray hair, looked up with relief when she spotted the two volunteers. "We're really shorthanded today," she explained. "I've got a supply list a mile long, and there are ten patients in occupational therapy who are going to come back to unmade beds unless we work fast."

Bernie nodded. "Okay," she said, taking the requisition slips from the nurse and handing them to Shelley. "Beds are my specialty, I'm afraid. Why don't you go down to Central Supplies, Shell?"

Shelley, who didn't really like making beds, agreed quickly. "Sure," she said, glancing at the number of items on the lists and whistling. "If this takes as long as I think it will, you'll have all those beds made before I can get back to help.'' She smiled mischievously. ''At least I hope so!''

As she started off down the hall, Bernie headed for the supply closet where she found stacks of fresh sheets, towels, and blankets. While she worked, she couldn't help remembering Roger's bed-making lesson. As she smoothed the bottom sheet, seam-side down across the mattress, she could still hear the frustrated nurse scolding and the other volunteers giggling. Thank goodness Roger won't have to go through that anymore, she thought.

When the bed was as perfect as she could get it, with the top sheet loosened so the patient could stretch out his or her toes, Bernie moved on to the next bed. Smoothly and efficiently, she finished bed after bed until she had started the window bed in the last room. It was after four when Shelley poked her head in and Bernie told her, ''Good Shell, you're just in time to help me with the door bed.''

Together, the girls made short work of the final bed. Hoping to visit with Minette and her mother, they started for the desk. But the floor nurse met them with a new list in her hand. ''Finished?'' she asked. ''Great! Here are some more supplies we need, and the water has to be done.''

Bernie and Shelley sighed, then headed for the Unit's kitchenette. They laid a clean towel from the supply closet on the tray of a steel cart, then loaded it with fresh water pitchers for each bed. As they wheeled the cart out into the hall, they nearly collided with a tall, sandy-haired young man in a maroon jacket.

''Roger!'' Shelley backed the cart away just in time. ''Where on earth are you going in such a hurry?''

''Hi, you two.'' Roger grinned, stepped aside, then kept walking. ''Can't talk now,'' he told them. ''I've got to get these papers downstairs to Admitting. It's my last official duty on the Paper Patrol.''

"Your last duty?" asked Bernie. "Wait, Rog. What do you mean?"

"Can't stop," he told her, over his shoulder. "I've got a new job. See you!" Without another word, he strode off down the hall, headed for the elevators. Bernie stared after him.

"What do you think *that* was all about?" she asked.

"I guess he'll tell us after work," Shelley said. "He sure looked happy," she added.

"So does a certain little girl in the next room," said Bernie. She had pushed the water cart on to the next door, where a tiny figure was dancing up and down with excitement. Minette put her arms around Bernie and greeted her with a great big hug.

"Hi, Minette," Bernie said. "How's our runaway?"

"Hey," said Shelley, getting a hug, too, "we have a surprise for you."

Minette paused. "Huh?" she asked.

"A surprise," Bernie repeated. "Oh, dear," she said, "I wish Nick were here, so we could tell her in French."

"You know, a surprise," Shelley coached. "Something that goes . . ." She put her hands over Minette's eyes, then took them away. "BOOM!" she said in a loud voice.

Minette laughed, then looked confused. "Huh?" she said again.

"There's only one thing to do," Bernie told Shelley. "We'll just have to show her. You give Mrs. Charpentier her water, and I'll go get the Thanksgiving treats." She walked off down the hall and came back a few minutes later to find Minette on Shelley's lap. They were laughing and making signs to each other while Mrs. Charpentier looked on.

"Here it is!" Bernie announced, carrying in the white

99

pastry box from Sheridan's. "There's one for you and one for your mom." She put the box on Mrs. Charpentier's bed tray and opened it up. Inside were the beautifully decorated tarts.

Minette and her mother had eaten half their tarts before Bernie remembered. "We're missing someone," she said.

"Who?" asked Shelley, brushing pie crust crumbs from her lap.

"Why, Mrs. B, of course," Bernie told her. "Let's finish the water, and see if we can get permission to bring a visitor down from Long Term."

"Bernie, that's a great idea," Shelley said, putting Minette gently on the foot of her mother's bed. "We'll be right back, Minette," she said, holding up one finger. "Wait right here."

The two volunteers finished putting fresh water beside almost every bed on the unit, greeting the patients, chatting with those who were lonely. Even the patients whose diet lists were marked "NPO" got a friendly smile or a joke. Then, when everything was done, and the old pitchers had been stacked on the kitchenette's dumbwaiter for the trip to Dietary's dishwasher, they went to the floor nurse.

The slender woman listened to them, then thought for a moment. "I guess that would be all right," she said. "You say Mrs. Bandler speaks French?"

"Yes," said Shelley. "And the doctor wants her to get a lot of walking in."

Within minutes, the two had gone up to Long Term and gotten permission to bring Mrs. B for a visit. As soon as they stepped off the elevator and rounded the corner with their friend, Minette spotted them. She raced over to Mrs. Bandler. After a giant hug and kiss, the two were talking away as though they'd known each other for years.

The girls introduced Mrs. Bandler to Minette's mother, and in no time the three of them were talking French so

100

fast that Bernie had to laugh. "I think we need subtitles," she told Shelley as she watched their excited faces.

"Well, as chairman of the refreshment committee," Shelley said, "I vote we go get that other pastry box." She went to the desk and retrieved the other surprise they'd brought from Sheridan's. When Harriet Bandler opened the little box and saw the initialed tart her friends had made for her, her eyes misted over. "Why, girls," she said. "This is about the most elegant dessert I've ever seen."

"The elegant part," Shelley told her, "is thanks to Nichole. But the delicious part is my pumpkin filling. Try it!"

"Mmmmmmmmm!" Mrs. Bandler said as soon as she'd swallowed the first bite. Before long, the tart was finished and Mrs. Bandler was closing the box and helping the girls clean up. "My," she told them, "that was delicious. And just the right size." She smiled. "After all, I am in training."

"Training?" asked Bernie.

"For my guest lecture tomorrow," Mrs. Bandler told her. "I want to look my best for your History Club."

"I can't wait!" exclaimed Shelley. "Mr. Haggerty has hired a bus and everything!"

Bernie smiled at their friend. "Are you nervous, Mrs. B?" she asked.

"You bet I am!" Mrs. Bandler told them. "But I just keep reminding myself that all that nervous energy means I'm alive." She shook her head, her eyes shining. "And I'd rather be nervous than bored any day!"

With their work done, the volunteers said good-bye to Minette and her mom, checked out with the floor nurse, and then walked Mrs. Bandler back to her room. When they'd taken the elevator to the main floor, Roger met

101

them at the Volunteer Office. "Ready to walk home?" he asked.

"Sure," said Bernie. "And we're ready to hear all about this new job of yours." She signed out on the duty roster behind Mrs. Hurley's desk, then headed for the front door. "What are you going to be doing?"

"You'll see for yourself," he told her. "I start on Thanksgiving Day."

"Come on, Rog," Shelley begged. "Give us a hint." She took her sweater and purse out of her locker and followed her friends. "Is it damage-proof?"

"Yep." He grinned. "And I'll be able to do what I do best," he told them proudly. The girls teased him all the way down Dale Avenue and all along Farview until they got to his house. But Roger wasn't budging. "I'm not telling you any more," he said, enjoying their suspense. "You'll just have to wait and see." He waved, then walked up his driveway and through his front door.

"Who needs this?" asked the big boy at the back of the bus the next day. His face was twisted into a frown and his voice was angry and deep. "Who needs to listen to some old bat talk about yesterday's news?"

"Jeffrey Spellman," Bev said, turning in her seat to confront the loudmouth, "if you didn't want to hear Mrs. Bandler, why on earth did you sign up for this trip?"

"Hey," Jeffrey chuckled, "it gets us out of eighth period, doesn't it?" He crossed his long legs, sticking them out into the middle of the aisle, then grinned at the students seated around him. "Why else do you figure half these people are here, Madame Vice President?" He looked around the bus. Almost every seat was filled. "Or did you think the History Club had suddenly gotten popular?"

"Well," said Nichole, from her seat beside Bev, "it's

going to be popular after today. Mrs. B makes history really exciting.''

"Right," said Jeffrey sarcastically, "and after today, I'm going to give up my flying lessons and spend all my time reading history books!" Several students laughed. Everyone at school knew two things about Jeffrey: he was a bully and he loved flying. In fact, that was about all they knew, since most people were too afraid of him to make friends.

Mr. Haggerty heard the laughter. He stood up from his seat behind the driver. "What's going on back there?" he asked. He was a small, wiry man with pale hair who wore such brightly colored shirts that students had started calling him "Flash" behind his back. Now, he peered toward the commotion. "Need some help?"

"No thanks, Mr. Haggerty," Bev told him. "Everything's fine."

"Yes, indeedy, Mr. H," Jeffrey sang out. "We're just all so eager to hear about World War Two!" He turned to the others. "Right, gang?" he asked in a big, phony voice.

Some of the students sang out, "Sure!" "That's right!" Others were embarrassed at his antics, but too afraid to object. Not Shelley. Seated beside Bernie, she turned on Jeffrey. "Look, Mr. Big Shot," she scolded. "Mrs. Bandler happens to be a friend of mine." Her brown eyes flashed.

Bernie backed her up. "Mine, too." She pictured the funny, clever old woman, and decided that her classmates would love Mrs. Bandler as much as she did. "But who cares what Jeffrey says, anyway?"

"I care," insisted Shelley. "What gives this bully the right to talk about someone he doesn't even know?"

"And what gives you the right, little girl," Jeffrey

103

asked, leaning across the aisle to face Shelley, "to get so cute when you're mad?"

"Give me a break!" Shelley turned away, her arms folded tight around herself. "Get lost, Spellman," she said.

"I wouldn't talk that way if I were you," said Jeffrey threateningly. He leaned over closer to Shelley, putting his face next to hers.

"And if I were you," said a voice behind Jeffrey, "I wouldn't go pushing my way into places where I'm not wanted."

"Who says?" Jeffrey turned around, half rising from his seat.

"I say." Roger stood up, his hands on his hips. He didn't take his steady gray eyes off Jeffrey. And, with his long legs and slender, athlete's build, he was at least four inches taller than the chunky bully. The kids seated around the two boys held their breath, then looked toward the front of the bus to see if Mr. Haggerty had heard the argument. But he was talking to the driver and didn't even look up.

Suddenly Jeffrey Spellman seemed a lot less ready for a fight than he had been a second before. He looked at Roger, then put his hands in the pockets of his baseball jacket. "Well, if it isn't Mr. Jock," he said. "When your arm gets better, give me a call and we'll go a few rounds." He sat back down in his seat and didn't speak again for the rest of the ride.

"Great," Bernie told Roger, as she and Teddy climbed down off the bus behind him. "Now you've got the biggest bully in the school hot under the collar."

"No prob," Teddy assured her. "I was right there with my man, Roger. If Jeffrey had decked him, I would have taken Shelley and run!"

"I couldn't help it, Bern," her friend insisted. "He was hassling Shelley."

104

"I know." Bernie watched the group heading for the entrance of Mercy. "I just hope he doesn't decide to hassle Mrs. B!"

"From what you've told us about your Mrs. B," Roger said, "she can take care of herself."

Bernie spotted Jeffrey Spellman in the group, his hands still in his pockets, his head lowered angrily. "I hope so," she said. "I certainly hope so."

As everyone took a seat in the crowded waiting room off Long Term Care, Nichole leaned over to whisper to Shelley. "Doesn't it feel strange to be here out of uniform?" she asked.

Shelley looked around the room, wondering where Mrs. B was. "It sure does," she agreed. "But if we feel strange, imagine how our guest speaker must be feeling about now."

"That's right," said Bernie. "She was pretty nervous yesterday." She, too, surveyed the packed room. "I hope she didn't change her mind."

But Mrs. Bandler hadn't changed her mind. And all three girls realized it when a smartly dressed, elderly woman in street clothes met Mr. Haggerty at the front of the room. They hardly recognized Mrs. Bandler out of her bathrobe! Her hair was combed back from her face, and she wore a pretty, navy blue dress with a matching jacket. She shook their teacher's hand with confidence, then turned, smiling, to the Ridge Dale students.

"Hello," she said. "I'm Harriet Bandler. I was a Red Cross nurse stationed in France during the Second World War." She studied the sea of faces in front of her, and winked when she spotted her three friends in the second row. "I guess that makes me kind of a living fossil," she said with a laugh. "So I think you all ought to ask me as many questions as you can.

"But first, I'd like to tell you a little bit about what we did in the base camps and what wartime medicine was like." As she talked, the boys and girls leaned forward intently from their chairs. Her stories were as exciting as ever, and soon students were asking, "What happened next?" "What did you do then?" "How did you get out of that one?"

All except one student. From the beginning, Jeffrey Spellman was restless. He turned in his seat, made faces at friends, and finally, when everyone was too interested in what Mrs. Bandler was telling them to pay him any attention, he began interrupting her. "Big deal!" he sneered loudly when she was describing how the Red Cross set up a hospital in Normandy after D day. "You missed the real action, grannie!"

Mr. Haggerty stood up from his seat in the front row. "That will be enough," he said, turning red in the face. Clearly he was too young and too new to deal with a bully like Jeffrey.

But Mrs. Bandler wasn't. She stared at Jeffrey for a moment, then told him firmly, "I don't have grandchildren, young man." She put her hand up to the pretty sapphire-colored locket she wore around her neck. "But if I did, they wouldn't be as rude as you are."

Several students applauded, then Mrs. Bandler continued her story. But Jeffrey hadn't given up. Every chance he got, he caused some kind of disturbance. Sometimes he coughed loudly and continuously. Sometimes he yawned noisily. Finally, when Mrs. Bandler was telling them about a nurse who performed a complicated operation by following the instructions of a wounded doctor, he interrupted again. "Come on," he said. "You got this stuff from a soap opera." He looked around the room for support. "She's making this up!"

Mrs. Bandler walked to where she could see Jeffrey more clearly. "Young man," she said, "what is your name?"

"Jeffrey," he told her. "But you can call me Jeff."

"All right, Jeff," Mrs. Bandler said. "Would it help if I gave you some specifics? My memory isn't the best, but I'll try to answer any questions you ask."

"Okay," Jeffrey challenged her. "For starters, how about the name of this wonder nurse."

"She wasn't a wonder nurse, Jeff," Mrs. Bandler said. "She was just following orders. And her name was Harriet Bandler."

"It was her!" Shelley gasped. "It was Mrs. B!" The whole group was surprised and delighted to find out they'd been listening to a real, live heroine. Hands shot up all over the room, as student after student had more questions to ask. "What was it really like when bombs fell?" "What happened when you didn't have enough supplies for all your patients?" "Did you ever give up?"

Mrs. Bandler smiled and raised her hands. "One at a time," she begged. "I'll answer everyone. That's what I'm here for." She talked on and on until it was long past the time Mr. Haggerty had set for the bus to leave. That's when Jeffrey found a new way to sabotage Mrs. Bandler.

"It's time to go, Mr. H," he announced, pointing to his watch. "Mr. Bus Driver is waiting!"

But Mr. Haggerty had seen the excitement in the room. "How many vote to extend this meeting of the History Club by fifteen minutes?" he asked. Before he could finish the question, every hand in the room was raised. Every hand but Jeffrey's. "I've got to go, Mr. H," he said in a whiny, cartoon voice. "My mommy needs me at home."

Mr. Haggerty had reached his limit. "Jeffrey," he said, walking up to the heavyset boy and taking him by the arm, "if you have to leave, allow me to help you out right now."

"Oh, please don't," Mrs. Bandler asked from the front of the room. Both Mr. Haggerty and Jeffrey turned around, surprised. "I've gotten kind of used to his background noise.

It reminds me of the Germans' V-1 bombs." She shook her head, smiling. "We used to call them buzz bombs."

"Buzz bombs?" Jeffrey asked.

"Sure," Mrs. Bandler told him. "The Germans had Stuka bomber planes, light planes that would dive in low and try to destroy our bases."

"Yeah," said Jeffrey. "Dive bombers. I've read about those."

"Well, reading about them and having them coming at you are two different things," Mrs. Bandler said.

Jeffrey was paying attention. Really paying attention. He stopped in his tracks and turned to face Mrs. Bandler. "Didn't the Luftwaffe use jet planes, too?"

Mrs. Bandler smiled. "I see you really know your planes, Jeff," she said. She looked at the other students. "For those of you who aren't the aircraft experts Jeff here is, the Luftwaffe was the German air force. And yes, Jeff, toward the end of the war, they did use jet fighters." She grinned at him. "Thank goodness they didn't start earlier, or it might have changed history."

"Did you ever see one of our B-17s?" Jeffrey asked next.

"I sure did," Mrs. Bandler told him. "Several of those Flying Fortresses flew out of a base where I was stationed."

"Wow!" Jeffrey walked toward her. "What were they like?" His face was eager, expectant. "Were they bigger than a B-24?"

"Well, let me see . . ." Mrs. Bandler tried to remember. "They flew B-24s over Tours. That was before the German military hid the bomb under Hitler's desk."

"A bomb under Hitler's desk!" A boy in the back row raised his hand. "Did it go off?"

"It sure did," said Mrs. Bandler. "But I guess that's a

whole new story." She looked at Mr. Haggerty. "Maybe we should save it for another meeting?"

"When?" "When can we come back?" Eager voices all across the room made it clear that the History Club had just gotten a new lease on life. Mr. Haggerty, grinning broadly, raised his hands for quiet.

"Okay, everyone," he announced. "We have to call a halt for today. But we'll set up another meeting with Mrs. Bandler. Meanwhile, let's give her a hand and then form a line for the bus."

As the whole group broke into loud applause, Mrs. Bandler smiled. "Thanks for coming," she told them. "You brightened my whole day."

Bernie and her gang rushed to the front of the room. "You were amazing!" the redheaded JV told her, hugging her tight.

"Have you signed a movie contract yet?" asked Teddy. Laughing, the girls introduced Roger and Teddy to Mrs. Bandler, but their talk was interrupted by Mr. Haggerty. "I'm sorry," he told them, "but we really have to go now." He led the way to the bus, but as she waved good-bye to Mrs. Bandler, Bernie noticed one student lag behind.

It was Jeffrey Spellman! He waited until he and Mrs. Bandler were the only ones in the room. "Do you think I could come visit you sometime?" he asked, shyly. "I mean, I'm sorry about acting like a jerk, and I'd really like to talk about warplanes with someone who actually saw them."

"Of course, you can visit," Mrs. Bandler told him. "On one condition." She paused, then smiled warmly. "You'll take me flying one day."

Jeffrey grinned. "You bet," he said. "I'll even teach you how to do loops!"

10

"Thanks for Everything, God!"

It was Thanksgiving morning. No school! But even though most of the students at Ridge Dale High were snoozing snugly in their beds, Bernie was up by eight. She knew that today was one of the longest, loneliest days of the year for hospital patients. While their families sat around the holiday table, they were forced to stay in bed, waiting for a phone call or an evening visit.

By eight-thirty, Bernie was dressed in her JV tunic. But as soon as she got downstairs, she realized someone had gotten up even earlier than she had. She walked into the kitchen and stood still, enjoying the rich, warm smells of Thanksgiving dinner baking. "Mmmmm!" she said. "I can't wait until three o'clock!"

"Well, Virgil won't be ready before that," Mrs. O'Connor told her. She opened the oven door and squeezed gravy onto the huge bird with a baster. "He needs to take his time."

Bernie smiled. "Mom," she asked, "why do we always name our turkeys?"

Her mother closed the oven door and put down the baster. "I don't know," she said. "Grandma always did it, so I do, too." She laughed. "When I was in school, we had to translate Virgil's poetry from Latin. Since he gave me such a hard time, I thought this year I'd put him on the hot seat!"

Bernie walked to the refrigerator and took out the glass pitcher of orange juice. Suddenly, she had an idea. "Could I name the turkey next year, Mom?"

"Sure, I guess so, dear." She saw the mischievous twinkle in her daughter's green eyes. "Anyone in mind yet?"

Bernie poured herself a tall glass of juice. "Yep," she said. "I'd like to name next year's turkey Jeffrey Allen Spellman."

Mrs. O'Connor considered the suggestion. "Well," she said, folding her arms and tilting her head to one side, "it doesn't sound quite as elegant as Virgil. Are you sure he deserves it?"

Bernie remembered the way the school bully had interrupted Mrs. B's talk, the way he'd called her "grannie." She grabbed a coat from the hook by the door and slipped into it. "I'm sure," she said, grinning, then waved and started off for Mercy.

She met Shelley and Nichole at the corner, and the three of them walked on to Roger's. He was waiting for them at the end of his driveway, wearing his new maroon blazer under his JV football jersey. Tucked under one arm, he carried a big black box. "Hi," he said. "Ready for Thanksgiving?"

"You should smell my house," Bernie told him. "Mom's going all out this year!"

"Yeah," Roger said. "By the number of places my

111

mom has set at the table, it looks like we're feeding an army!''

Shelley laughed. ''Well, I was smart enough to burn up our stove this year, so Dad and I are eating out!'' She loved the holidays when her father didn't have to work and the two of them could spend time together.

''I wish *we* could eat out,'' Nichole told them. ''Mother gave Cook the day off, and she's trying to make dinner herself.'' Her pretty nose wrinkled in disgust. ''I think I better stop at Sheridan's on the way home and pick up emergency supplies!''

''Speaking of Sheridan's,'' Shelley said, ''Elise told me the hospital truck picked up our pies yesterday.'' She grinned at her three friends. ''So I hereby invite you all to the snack bar after work today. My treat!''

''Well,'' considered Bernie, ''I should get home to help Mom.'' She slipped her arm through Shelley's. ''But I can always be talked into extra calories!''

''Me, too,'' Nichole told them. ''Especially if my mother's going to fix her wheat germ and tuna soufflé!''

The four JVs chattered all the way to Mercy. As they turned onto Hospital Drive, Nichole noticed the box Roger was carrying. ''What's in there?'' she asked.

Roger glanced down at the black box. ''Just some equipment for my assignment at Mercy,'' he said.

Shelley laughed. ''Roger is keeping his new job under wraps. Don't bother trying to get any details out of him. He won't budge.''

The friends walked through the big front door of Mercy and down the hall to the Volunteer Office. Everywhere they looked, they saw bright paper decorations on the walls. There were turkeys and orange pumpkins and stalks of wheat. Tied above the door to Mrs. Hurley's office were three ears of brightly colored Indian corn. The silver-haired Director greeted them warmly. ''Happy Thanksgiving,

112

team," she said. "Thanks for waking up so early on a holiday.

"Now, let me see." She considered the four teens. "I think we'll need Nichole's help with all the Thanksgiving bouquets that are backed up in the flower room." She handed the duty roster to Nichole, who signed her name and wrote in 'flower room' beside it. "And Shelley, I need you in Peeds today." Shelley was delighted. She loved working on the Pediatrics Unit, and couldn't wait to play games and read books with Mercy's youngest patients.

"Bernie," Mrs. Hurley continued, scanning the attendance charts in front of her, "it seems Long Term Care and Med-Surg are both shorthanded today. Do you think you could split your time?"

Bernie smiled. "Sure," she agreed. "Can I finish up in Long Term?" She already had special Thanksgiving plans for Mrs. B!

"As for you, Mr. Thornton," Mrs. Hurley said, "we're going to put your idea in operation today."

"What?" Bernie looked at Roger. "What idea?"

"Didn't he tell you?" asked the Volunteer Director. "Roger's come up with a wonderful new Recreational Therapy program for our Hemo patients."

"You did?" Shelley was impressed. She knew how bored the kidney patients got, coming two or three times a week to the hospital for hemodialysis, a blood-cleansing procedure that lasted four or five hours. "What's your program, Rog?"

Roger put down the box, grinning. "Why don't you come and see for yourself after work?" he asked. He signed the roster, then tucked the box under his arm again and headed for the elevator. "I've got to get started now." As she watched him go, Bernie thought she'd never seen him look so confident and happy before.

* * *

As she gave out the menus on Med-Surg, Bernie made sure to stay extra long with the patients who needed to talk. One woman's husband and children were visiting her ill mother three states away. "Gee, I miss them," she told Bernie. "Especially today."

"Well, I know it's not the same as being with your family, but at least the doctor took you off dietary restrictions today." Bernie glanced down the list of foods on the menu she'd just given the woman. "That means you can have turkey with all the trimmings!"

"I thought something smelled good," the woman said. "This will be my first regular meal since my surgery." She checked off turkey and mashed potatoes and peas on the menu.

Bernie took the menu back, slipping it onto the clipboard she carried. "That calls for a celebration," she said. She looked at the items the woman had checked off. "You forgot cranberry sauce," she said, "and pumpkin pie." She handed the clipboard back. "How can you celebrate without pumpkin pie?"

The woman pulled up her sheets with one hand and took the clipboard back with the other. "Do you really think I could?" she asked.

Bernie double-checked the diet list for the floor. "You sure can," she said.

The woman brightened. "Then let's go all the way," she said, checking off the dessert. "Will you come back to help me celebrate?"

"Sure," Bernie told her. She left wondering how she was going to manage going back and forth between two units all morning!

After she had done the water on Med-Surg, it was time for Bernie to go to Long Term. As she hurried off the elevator and picked up the diet list from the Long Term desk, she was surprised to hear voices coming from Mrs. Bandler's room. Did their friend have a family after all?

Quietly, she peeked into the room. There were Mrs. Charpentier, Minette, and Mr. Haggerty! "Hi," she said, as everyone looked up. "Happy Thanksgiving."

"Hello, dear," Mrs. Bandler greeted her. "Come on in and sit down." She looked around the room, as Minette raced to hug Bernie. "If you can find a chair, that is!"

Mr. Haggerty stood up. "That's all right, Mrs. Bandler," he said. "I really have to be going, anyway." He leaned down and took her hand in his. "I just wanted to make sure my star speaker was going to be ready for our next meeting."

"I certainly will," Mrs. Bandler told him, smiling. "As long as you don't mind holding it in the nursing home. I'm being discharged tomorrow."

Bernie was amazed. "You are?"

"Yes, dear," Mrs. Bandler explained. "It seems talking with you young people agrees with me. The doctors here can't find a single reason for me to be in a hospital, anymore. And they think I may even be able to move back into my apartment soon!"

"That's wonderful!" Bernie told her. "Now we can visit you in your own room."

"Or at school," Mr. Haggerty added. He was wearing a bright yellow shirt with broad green stripes, and Bernie smiled as she thought to herself that he certainly deserved his nickname. "I'm trying to talk Mrs. Bandler into teaching part-time for our history department."

"That's right. We're even talking about working on a textbook." Mrs. Bandler winked at Bernie. "A new kind of book that would make history a little more . . . that is, not quite so . . ."

"Boring," Mr. Haggerty finished for her. He smiled at

115

his new friend. "Until I met Mrs. Bandler, I'd forgotten just how exciting history can be."

Bernie looked around the room full of people, and at the lively old woman everyone had come to see. She could hardly believe this was the lonely Mrs. Nobody she'd met a few short weeks ago! "Whatever you're teaching, Mrs. B," she said, "I'm taking! Consider me signed up in advance!"

Everyone laughed, and waved good-bye as Mr. Haggerty left. Then Minette and Mrs. Charpentier pulled up his chair for Bernie. The four of them were giggling and gossiping, when a new visitor peeked through the door. It was Jeffrey Spellman!

"Hi," he said shyly. "Just thought you might need company on Thanksgiving." He looked around the crowded room. "But I guess you don't." Embarrassed, he began to leave.

"Just one minute, young man." Mrs. Bandler called Jeffrey back with the same stern tone she'd used at her "lecture." But when he turned around to face her, he saw that she was smiling broadly. "There's no such thing as too much company on Thanksgiving. March right back in here!"

This day was certainly full of surprises, Bernie thought, as she watched a meek, happy Jeffrey join them. And, as she saw the way the ex-bully played with Minette and joked with Mrs. B, she also decided she'd have to find a new name for next year's turkey!

After a visit that seemed all too short, Bernie did the water on the rest of the Long Term Care Unit and returned to the woman recovering on Med-Surg. Over her Thanksgiving dinner, the woman talked cheerfully. "Either this turkey is delicious," she said, "or it's been so long since I've had a normal meal, I've forgotten what real food tastes like!"

Bernie thought of the wonderful meal waiting for her at home. "Maybe it's a bit of both," she laughed. She noticed that Dietary had tried really hard to make the Thanksgiving trays festive. The cranberry sauce was garnished with orange slices, and the pumpkin pie was sprinkled with cinnamon. "My mouth is beginning to water," she told the woman. "Why don't I take these dishes away while you finish your dessert?"

"Miss?" The patient looked up from her meal.

"Yes?" Bernie said, turning back from the door.

"Thanks," the woman told her, smiling. "You don't know how good it is to have someone to talk to."

Bernie felt wonderful. Now she knew why she'd jumped out of her warm bed this morning! She collected the rest of the lunch trays and before she knew it, it was time to sign out. By twelve thirty-five, she was downstairs at the Volunteer Office. Shelley and Nichole met her right outside Mrs. Hurley's door.

"Let's go," urged Nichole. "I'm dying to see Roger in action!"

The three of them turned down the hall and walked toward the wing where outpatients came for hemodialysis. "He's been on duty here all morning," said Shelley as they neared the unit. "I hope nothing's broken!"

"Nope," said Bernie, looking into a big, sunny room where several men and a small boy lay on beds beside dialysis machines. They were attached to the machines by catheters, and while they lay there, their blood was passed through filters and purified—something their own kidneys were too weak to do. "Everything looks fine."

In fact, things looked better than fine. Instead of the quiet checker or card games that Hemo patients usually played during their treatment, these people were staring intently at a giant TV screen in the front of the room. Suddenly, they all broke into applause. "Wow!" said one of the men, "that was a great play!"

The screen went dark and the lights came on. That was

117

when the girls saw Roger! He was seated up front, beside the TV. "That was our third game of the season," he explained to the patients. "Did you see the way the end went wide? That's what Coach calls our Impossible Split." He shook his head, smiling. "It shouldn't be possible, but it works every time!"

"Can we watch another game?" A small red-haired boy, who looked like an older version of Bernie's brother Matt, looked pleadingly at Roger. "Just one more?"

Roger laughed. "There's not enough time," he said. "Your treatment's almost finished."

"Already?" the little boy asked, surprised. "It usually takes a lot longer."

"No, it doesn't," said a nurse who came in to remove his catheter and put away the machine. "It just seems like that because you're usually not having so much fun."

One of the men sat up, straightening his shirt and reaching for his jacket as soon as the nurse had undone his catheter. "Thanks, Roger," he said. "This was the best idea yet. I really enjoyed going over those plays with you."

"Me, too," said another man, stretching his legs. "It makes this routine a lot easier to put up with."

"Can we watch more games next time?" the boy begged.

"I think we better," the nurse told Roger, smiling, "or we'll have a mutiny on our hands."

Roger looked very happy. "Of course," he said. "I've got lots more football films." He took a videotape out of the VCR. "And Coach told me he might even stop by." Roger grinned at the men. "If you don't mind some strong language when the calls go against Ridge Dale, you'll get some expert commentary."

"Terrific!" One of the men shook Roger's hand. "It's a date."

Now Roger saw the girls. He waved, then put his tapes

back into the box and joined them. "Okay," he told the patients, "see you next week!"

"Bye!" The little boy waved. "Bye Mr. Roger, see you soon!"

"Well," said Shelley, as the four friends headed back to the Volunteer Office, "I guess Mrs. B isn't the only hit around here."

"Gosh, Rog," said Bernie. "What an incredible idea!"

Roger smiled. He still remembered the excitement on the little boy's face. "Yeah," he said. "I wanted to call the program *Armchair Football,* but Mrs. Hurley says it's too good to limit to sports. We can have a lot of different visiting experts.

"I already talked to Teddy, and he's crazy about the idea of coming in with his collection of classic movies." Roger shook his head. "The only problem is how to keep him quiet long enough for the patients to watch the movies!"

"Maybe I could show our films of Paris," suggested Nichole. She remembered the videotapes her father had taken two summers ago. "Of course, the styles would be hopelessly out of date," she said.

"I don't think that would matter one bit," Roger told her as they signed out on the roster. "It's a great idea. And I hope you'll have lots of company. Mrs. Hurley says she'll be able to recruit a lot of volunteers who don't want to go on hospital units to give talks like mine." He smiled shyly. "She visited Hemo today, and she said she's never seen the patients so involved."

"You were right, Rog," Bernie told him. "Your new job *does* let you use what you know best." She was proud that her friend had found a way at last to use his talent at Mercy. "I never thought football could do that much good!"

"Hey," Roger warned, "that's my favorite sport you're talking about."

"That's just what I mean," Bernie explained. "Most

119

people think of football as a sport. Who would have dreamed that it could be such good medicine, too?''

The four teens had already found a table by the window at the hospital snack bar before Bernie remembered. ''Wait a minute,'' she said, jumping up from her seat. ''We forgot someone.''

Minutes later, she was back with Mrs. Bandler. ''Mrs. B!'' Nichole hugged her. ''Look who's here, everyone!''

''The hit of the History Club!'' exclaimed Shelley, getting up to give Mrs. Bandler another hug. ''I'm treating my cooking team to dessert. Will you have some with us?''

''You bet I will,'' Mrs. Bandler said, sitting between Roger and Nichole. ''That is if you don't mind an old fossil joining you.''

''Mind?'' asked Roger. ''We'd be honored.'' He grinned. ''That is, if you don't mind eating with four loud teenagers!''

''Make that three loud teenagers,'' said Nichole. ''As for me, I'm just going to sit here feeling happy.'' She sighed contentedly, then dug into the pumpkin pie the waitress brought her.

''What happened, Nick?'' Shelley asked.

''Nothing really big,'' the pretty JV told her. ''I guess you'd have to say a lot of little things. I think I've figured out what Mercy is all about.''

Bernie looked at her. ''What do you mean?''

''Well,'' Nichole told them, ''when I rushed down to Ortho for that Code Nine the other day, it was because I wanted something exciting to happen.''

Mrs. Bandler shook her head. ''You certainly weren't going to settle for anything less than saving a life, were you?'' she asked, smiling.

Nichole smiled back. ''You wanted us to be patient, but I wanted a big adventure. And I actually got it.'' She took a sip of her soda, then continued. ''Don't get me wrong. I'm so glad we found Minette and that everything worked

120

out." She paused, then touched Mrs. Bandler's arm gently. "But Mrs. B is right. That's not what working at Mercy means. You can't have adventures like that every day."

"I hope not!" said Bernie, laughing. "Or I'd never pass math!"

But Nichole was serious. "The point is that most days at Mercy aren't full of big adventures. It's the little things that get you through.

"Like today. I was delivering all those gorgeous Thanksgiving floral arrangements, and I kept passing rooms with no meal trays. When I checked the diet lists, I found out they were all NPOs." Her blue eyes darkened. "Imagine not being able to eat or drink on Thanksgiving!

"I just had to do something," she told her friends. "So I took three flower arrangements that had been sent to patients who were already discharged. I tore them apart and put them together again. I made lots of little bouquets, just big enough to fit in Mercy's water pitchers, and delivered them to all the patients that couldn't eat today." She grinned. "I told them the rules said nothing by mouth, not nothing by nose!"

"What a lovely idea!" Mrs. Bandler said, putting down her fork. "What happened when you gave your bouquets out?"

"Oh," Nichole said, "nothing big." Her voice was quiet, happy. "Just smiles. Lots and lots of smiles."

As Bernie helped her mother finish setting the table, she wondered if she'd ever have room for Virgil or any of the other delicious food her mother had cooked. She wished she hadn't taken a second piece of pie at the snack bar!

"Here he is!" announced Mrs. O'Connor, as she came into the room with a huge platter. "Let's have a hand for Virgil!"

"Bravo! Bravo!" said Bernie's father, following with a carving knife and fork. "Places, everyone!"

121

In a twinkling, all the O'Connors were in their seats around the table. "Mmmmm!" said Matt, closing his eyes and rubbing his little stomach. "Scumshus!"

"That's scrumptious," Tracy corrected him. "I want white, Dad."

"I want dark," said Mr. O'Connor, as he prepared to carve.

"I'll take white, too," said Sara.

"Me, too," chimed in Kelly, who always followed the leader.

"I'll have dark," decided Bernie, who loved drumsticks. "How about you, Mom?"

"I want white," Mrs. O'Connor said. "And what would you like, Mathew?"

Bernie's little brother was puzzled. He looked at the faces around him, then at Virgil's golden crust. "Turkey!" he said. "Me want turkey!"

Everyone laughed, but after he'd finished carving, Bernie's father turned serious. "I'm not one for long prayers," he said. "But when I look around this table, I feel awfully grateful." He cleared his throat. "And since this is Thanksgiving, I think we should take just a minute to talk to God, each of us in our own way." He bowed his head, and one by one, Bernie saw her sisters and brother bow theirs. The usually noisy dining room grew silent.

It was hard to know where to start, Bernie thought. She had so much to be grateful for this Thanksgiving. Roger had found his own important place at Mercy. They had all found little Minette when it looked as if they wouldn't. Mrs. B had found that she loved teaching. And Bernie herself? She stole a glance at the bent heads around the table. She had found that there would never be enough time to say thank you for all her blessings! Finally, as she saw her family raise their heads and heard the cheerful sounds of laughter and plates being passed, she had just enough time to whisper quickly, "Thanks for everything, God!"